A MURDER IN WASHINGTON SQUARE

PENELOPE BANKS MURDER MYSTERIES
BOOK 5

COLETTE CLARK

DESCRIPTION

A little late-night mischief reveals a body...that promptly vanishes.

New York, 1925
Penelope "Pen" Banks and a few other zozzled young friends have decided to do something rather daring: break into the Washington Square Park Arch in an attempt to recreate the infamous affair of 1917.

Their impromptu party at the top is cut short by a violent thunderstorm. But not before Penelope glimpses, in a single flash of lightning, the body of a woman next to the fountain below.

By the time the partiers make it back down, the body has vanished.

In a case centered around Washington Square Park—where the students of New York University, patrons of the infamous Black and Tan saloons, bohemian artists of Greenwich Village, and entrenched old money collide—Penelope, now working even more closely with Detective Prescott and her usual set of friends, plans on finding exactly what happened that night.

A Body in Washington Square is the fifth book in the Penelope Banks Murder Mysteries series set in 1920s New York. The enjoyment of a historical mystery combined with the excitement, daring, and danger of New York during Prohibition and the Jazz Age.

AUTHOR'S NOTE

I like to make each of my books different to avoid falling into the rut of becoming predictable or boring or cliché. As such, this book begins in an unusual manner. Stick with it and pay close attention and I promise you'll find yourself with yet another interesting murder mystery filled with twists and turns. You'll also learn some very unusual, fun, and even a bit macabre facts about the history of Washington Square Park. Enjoy!

CHAPTER ONE

1925 WASHINGTON SQUARE PARK

"If you drop that bottle of gin, Ducky, I'll absolutely murder you."

"Not to worry, Pony, there's still plenty of champagne for you to drown in."

"Everyone knows Pony's poison is gin, not champagne," Bunny said in a droll voice.

"Chin, chin, chin, and a bottle of gin! It's half past ten, let the sinning begin!"

"Hush Ducky, are you trying to get us arrested before I've managed to pick the lock?" Pony protested.

"Just how much giggle juice did Ducky nip before this little escapade?" Bunny pondered aloud.

"Besides, it's more like four hours past ten."

"If Wooly knows what time it is, he obviously hasn't had enough giggle juice!"

"A good thing, since I'm the one holding the glasses," Wooly said, frowning at Ducky.

"Will the four of you hush? I need to concentrate on this lock."

"How much longer will you be, Pony? I thought you

knew how to pick a lock. I don't like the look of some of those people over there in the park."

"Calm your horses, Monkey, I'm almost there. It would help if Bunny held the flashlight straight. I swear there's no moon tonight!"

"It's just cloudy is all, might rain in fact."

"Thank you, for once again ruining the fun, Wooly," Bunny said dryly.

"I'm not ruining it, I'm just pointing out—"

"Got it!"

"Hurrah, Hurrah, our Pony has saved the day!"

"Close your head Ducky, or you'll land us all in the jug."

"Look at our Pony and her low hat slang," Bunny admired.

"Just a little something for Monkey to take home to daddums," Pony said with a grin.

"If he knew what I was involved in at the moment, *daddums* would have me on the next boat back to England and straight into a convent."

"You aren't Catholic, darling," Ducky said, looking confused.

"Exactly."

"Ugh, enough talk of fathers, religion, and celibacy, I'm not quite ossified enough for that," Bunny protested.

"I don't think I've ever seen you *completely* ossified, Bunny," Pony said.

"That's because, unlike Ducky, I can do it without waking the whole neighborhood."

"This is my neighborhood, I'll wake them all if I want."

"It won't be your neighborhood for long if you don't muzzle that trap," Pony said.

"Too late, it looks like one of his neighbors on The Row

has heard the ruckus. I just saw the lights come on," Wooly observed.

"Okay everyone, now that I have the door open, it's your last chance to say no. What we're doing is illegal, after all."

"Don't go getting morals now, Pony. The deed's already done, fingerprints and all."

"Pineapples!"

"Pony and her pineapples. When are you going to learn to curse like an adult, dove?"

"You're supposed to use her animal name, Bunny," Monkey reminded him.

"Whose idea was it to use animal names anyway?" Pony asked.

"Well, Ducky was already Ducky, he just hates doing anything by himself," Wooly said, sounding unimpressed.

"Speaking of which, while Pony is using her skirt to wipe the evidence, I'm heading in! Follow me, my merry band of criminals!"

"Watch your head, Ducky, that door is tiny!" Pony warned.

"Looks like it's pretty darn cozy inside as well," Bunny said, sticking his head in.

"How many steps do you think there are to the top of the arch?" Wooly asked.

"One, Two, Three—"

"No, no, no, Monkey, numbers are verboten. The same goes for you and your academic questions, Wooly," Bunny protested.

"Good, because I for one don't plan on counting how many drinks I have tonight."

"When have you ever, Ducky?"

"Thank you, Pony. Someone *finally* acknowledges my talents."

"Why are we doing this, again?" Monkey asked.

"Because we were all too young the last time this was done," Bunny said.

"Yes, but drinking was legal back then, and I heard that the door to get into the arch was unlocked at the time. That eliminates at least two crimes, I believe," Wooly said.

"That's what makes our adventure so much more daring. Just think of the lore!" Ducky sang.

"Can't we just leave it at a simple little party atop the arch and be done with it?" Pony suggested.

"Oh, look here's a small room. The perfect place to hold a real humdinger of a party the next time we do this. There are even openings looking down at the park," Ducky said.

"Perhaps we should get through this first time before we start talking about reunions," Pony hinted.

"Yes, yes, onward fearless soldiers! To the top of the Arch we go!"

"Ducky really is blotto, isn't he?" Bunny said with amusement.

"Will someone please watch him when we get to the top? I don't want him stumbling over the side right into the middle of Washington Square Park," Monkey said, worried.

"I've reached the top. Pony, be a dear and hold the gin while I open the hatch," Ducky said.

"Will do."

"Got it open! Out we go!"

"Careful, watch your step as you exit," Pony warned.

"My, what a divine view of New York! You can see right up 5th Avenue from here," Monkey sighed.

"Hello, New York!" Ducky shouted.

"Well, that'll certainly wake The Row," Bunny said dryly.

"It looks like Ducky's neighbors have even more lights on now," Wooly said, sounding worried.

"They're just having an all-night party like us," Ducky assured him.

"Wait, what was that?"

"What was what, Pony?"

"I thought I saw through the window...oh, never mind. I'm probably just ossified. Speaking of which, where is that gin?"

"Oh, was that a raindrop. Wooly was right, it's going to rain. My permanent!" Monkey cried.

"I thought you Brits were used to being soggy."

"I'm only half-British, and stop teasing, Bunny."

"A little champagne will make you forget all about your golden tresses, my sweet Monkey," Ducky cooed. "Who has the bottle?"

"Bunny, of course," Pony answered.

"Hop to it, dear boy before it does start to rain. There's nothing worse than watered-down bubbly," Ducky said.

"Done and done, old boy."

"Your attempt at a British accent needs work, Bunny," Monkey grumbled.

"Oh! That was a loud pop."

"Catch that foam in one of the glasses, Wooly. Let nothing go to waste!" Ducky shouted.

"Okay, to what should we toast?" Bunny asked.

"Ducky's return to the States," Pony said.

"Chin, chin!"

"Cheers!"

"And of course, bringing back his lovely bride-to-be, Monkey."

"Why thank you, Pony," Monkey said, her cheeks dimpling.

"Hear, hear! There, there! Where, where?"

"Oh, hush and drink, Ducky." Pony said with a laugh.

"It really is coming down harder isn't it?" Monkey said, worried.

"I find the rain refreshing, it's been so surprisingly warm this week."

"That's the spirit, Pony. Any true adventurer doesn't mind a little rain."

"Didn't you spend the last three years drinking your way around Europe, Ducky? That must have been quite the *daring* expedition."

"Oh Bunny, I did so miss your dry humor."

"You know, back in '17 when they did this, they declared all of Washington Square below us an independent country," Wooly noted.

"A fine idea! I hereby declare Washington Square Park the nation-state of...Duck-land!"

"Quack, Quack."

"No need to sound quite so sardonic, Bunny," Monkey said.

"Nonsense, in my newly christened Duckland, all are free to express themselves as they see fit. In fact, I shall shout it from—"

"Get down from there, you fool, you'll fall to your death!" Pony protested.

"You should also be quieter, Ducky. Pony was correct about this being illegal."

"Thank you for reminding us, Wooly," Bunny said, perfectly unconcerned. "Speaking of illegal, is there any more champagne?"

"Only a drop."

"Time to open the gin!" Ducky sang.

"Ugh, it's officially a storm now. This is no longer fun,

Ducky."

"At least share one glass of gin with us, Monkey," Pony pleaded.

"Oh, alright, one glass, I suppose."

"Yes, and you can tell Bunny and me how you and Ducky met. Wooly already knows the story."

"I'll definitely need the last of that champagne first."

"Don't be rude, Bunny."

"It's not a lack of manners, I'm just worried about the state of the bubbly with all this rain coming down."

"At any rate, getting to the story. Ducky and I were both —oh, was that lightning!"

"Yes, it was. We should probably all go down now," Wooly warned.

"And where did this torrent suddenly come from? That's me done, I'm going back down to that little room. This is no longer fun."

"I'll go with you, Monkey. I can't see anything through my glasses at this point," Wooly said.

"Should I go as a chaperone? Wouldn't want Wooly to tempt your Monkey with his, ahem, massive tusks."

"Oh, do hush, Bunny," Monkey scolded.

"I trust Wooly, he's a harmless old chap. Surely, you and Pony are brave enough to stay with me up top?"

"We're already soaked through, so we might as well."

"There's the spirit, Pony. So, now that it's only the three of us, allow me to be perfectly gauche and ask about this five million you inherited from our dearly departed Agnes Sterling. Now, *there's* something worth drinking to. When is the party?"

"Pony's been too busy solving murders around New York."

"Murders, you say? Ah yes, I heard about your old foe

Constance. Allow me to raise my glass to you. Way to purge your enemies, darling."

"I didn't murder her, and let's change the subject, please. This is supposed to be a fun homecoming, despite this heavy rain."

"Yes, New York, New York, my home sweet home!"

"Oh! That was a loud bit of thunder. Maybe Wooly was right about going inside," Pony suggested.

"Nonsense, that's just nature approving me as master of my domain!"

"Not so loudly, Ducky!"

"Oh let him be, Pony. What's the point of getting perfectly zozzled if you don't regret at least something in the morning?"

"I don't think—oh, there he goes!" Pony warned.

"At least he's facing the park this time. If he falls he won't give his neighbors a fright right at their front doors when they leave in the morning."

"Hello, people of Duckland! I am your king, I see you! I hear you!"

"Well, if that doesn't wake the rest of the neighborhood, I don't know what will. Get him down from there, Bunny! It's coming down in buckets now."

"Okay, here we go, Ducky. Ouch! Watch your arm," Bunny protested.

"I, swear, Ducky—*zounds*, what was that!"

"Don't lean over too far, Pony. I can only get one of you down at a time."

"I think I saw...oh, I'm not sure, it's so dark and this damnable rain."

"That was another flash of lightning. At this point, even I agree with Wooly, we should—"

"A body!" Pony announced.

"A what now?" Bunny asked, distractedly.

"A woman, she was lying there right by the fountain! Dead, I think."

"How can you tell? I can barely see the fountain in this storm. Looks like one of the lamps is out," Bunny said.

"I saw it when the lightning came. She's there, I swear it!"

"A dead body?" Ducky asked doubtfully.

"Don't look at me that way. We have to go down and make sure."

"Okay, okay. Back down the hatch," Ducky slurred.

"Watch yourself, Ducky. I'm not carrying you down these steps," Bunny warned.

"Quickly!"

"We're going as fast as we can, Pony," Bunny said.

"Ha! You lot certainly didn't last very long up there. Did you finally succumb to the rain?" Monkey teased.

"Pony saw a dead body by the fountain," Bunny teased right back.

"*A what?*"

"Ducky, you're going too slow—oh, catch him, Bunny!"

"Too late," Bunny sighed.

"Ducky! Are you all right, my darling?"

"His head is bleeding," Wooly observed.

"Pony, you go on. We'll deal with Ducky," Bunny urged.

"I can't get past him, these stairs are too narrow. Oh, I knew I should have gone back in first!"

"Are you sure she was dead, Pony? You have had quite a bit to drink."

"I know what I saw, Wooly. Bunny, can you please move Ducky so I can get past?"

"I read that you shouldn't move someone who has

suffered a head injury," Wooly said.

"She could still be alive!"

"Why was there a *dead body*?"

"Don't get hysterical, Monkey."

"Zounds! Can we please stop with these infernal animal names? This is serious! I have to see if she's all right."

"Okay, I've got him lucid...somewhat. Ducky? Ducky! Can you hear me? How many fingers am I holding up?" Bunny asked.

"If you could just shift him a bit..."

"Here, let me help," Wooly offered.

"Thank you, he's out of the way! You're the berries."

"What would a dead body be doing here at this time of night?"

"Welcome to New York, Monkey," Bunny said with a grin.

"Hurry now, everyone! Wait, I still have the bottle of gin in my hands. Oh, never mind, maybe it might do a bit of good if she's still—pineapples!"

"Hey, why'd you stop, Pony? We were—oh. Oh, no."

"Good evening, ma'am. Or should I say, good morning, considering the hour?"

"Ah...hello, officers."

"We've had a complaint of some disorderly conduct. Care to tell us what you are doing inside the Washington Square Park arch at two in the morning? How'd you even get in? Have you all been drinking? Wait, what's that in your hand?"

"This? It's—nothing."

"Nothing, huh?"

"Never mind what's in this bottle. It's a good thing you two officers are here. There is a dead woman over there by the fountain."

CHAPTER TWO

"I SWEAR SHE WAS HERE!" PENELOPE "PEN" BANKS (otherwise known as Pony) insisted, shouting over the rain which was once again mercilessly pelting them. She stared down at the ground near the fountain where she had seen the body of a woman from the top of the Washington Square Arch only a few minutes ago.

The heavy rain was enough to wash away any potential evidence from the scene. But surely it couldn't have gotten rid of an entire body?

"May the rest of us please go inside? Pony—I mean, *Penelope* is the only one who saw something. There's no reason we should drown in this rain."

The first officer shined a flashlight at Mona "Monkey" Harrington.

"The only place you five are going is down to the station with us."

"On what charge?" Derrick "Ducky" Bishop insisted in a foolishly indignant manner. He was still bleeding from where he'd bumped his head nearly falling down the staircase, and was ossified enough to supply a gin mill.

"How about trespass? Breaking and entering? Disorderly conduct?*Public drunkenness?*" The officer shined the light back towards Penelope. "And making a false report."

"It isn't a false report! In fact, I can tell you exactly what she looked like. She had red hair, was wearing a calf-length dark blue dress, though the rain probably darkened it some. It had a silver beaded design. She had on matching silver t-strap shoes."

"You saw that much from the top of the arch? In this darkness? With all this rain coming down? All while as sauced up as my mother's pot roast covered in gravy?"

"Yes, the flash of lightning made it more clear. I can also tell you I caught a glimpse of her inside that house over there." Pen pointed to the home they had all noted earlier, which was no longer showing any signs of life. "Alive."

Everyone turned to look at the house, one of the prestigious Greek Revival dwellings along "The Row," that bordered the north side of the park. With the windows dark again, it now looked as dead as the woman Penelope was certain she had seen. The looks on their faces when they turned back to her were understandably perplexed.

"Once again, care to tell me what's in the bottle, miss?" the second officer asked, shining his flashlight down toward the bottle she hadn't been able to inconspicuously rid herself of.

"I...mostly water by now."

"I see. And...were you drinking this '*mostly water*' before you supposedly saw a body?"

"I didn't imagine it, officer."

"You can explain it down at the station."

"You're arresting us?" Mona cried.

"That I am, miss."

This was bad. Very bad.

Despite this, Pen couldn't help but wonder what had happened to the woman's body.

She turned to look at the townhome situated on the outskirts of the park. Her eyes gravitated toward the window on the far right of the first floor. Those curtains hadn't been fully closed, and Pen had most definitely seen the red-headed woman arguing with someone just out of view right before he or she had slapped her. Right now, that window, along with all the others, was dark, curtains drawn. Still, she couldn't help but feel they were all being watched.

What had happened in that home? More importantly, what had happened to that woman?

―――――――

"I do believe this is a first for me, a ride in the back of a paddy wagon!"

"This isn't funny, Benjamin," Walter "Wooly" Adams scolded, futilely trying to wipe his glasses clear on his wet shirt.

"Tsk, tsk, it's Bunny, remember?" Benjamin "Benny" Davenport scolded right back with a smirk.

"Can we please stop with the animal names!" Mona cried, sobbing against the shoulder of her fiancé Ducky (who always went by Ducky).

"The charges are minor at best. When they find out who we are, they'll be inclined to let us go with nothing more than a wag of the finger. We should even get an apology for causing such an inconvenience to members of decent society over nothing more than a silly antic."

"That's right, Ducky, be sure to tell them who your family is. Don't forget to stick your nose as high in the air as possible. That will surely endear them to us," Benny said in a droll voice.

"Well, Pen certainly didn't help with her disappearing body. Perhaps it was a vampire? Or Frankenstein? Maybe it was Lazarus himself, back from the dead!"

"Oh do stop, Ducky, you're frightening me," Mona pleaded.

"Sorry, sweetums."

"Actually, Frankenstein was the doctor, not the monster," Walter said. "Many people who haven't read the book—"

"I didn't imagine it! I've seen a dead body before. At any rate, she didn't look to be in any condition where she could have simply woken up and walked away on her own. At the very least she was carried away by someone."

"But where?" Walter asked, the only one who didn't seem entirely doubtful of her claims. "And why?"

"I don't know! But I do know I saw her earlier in that house, the one whose lights came on during our little misadventure. I also saw her get slapped by someone. Perhaps a fight got out of hand." Pen turned to Ducky. "Do you know them? They're only a few houses down from yours."

Ducky frowned. "I only just returned this week, Pen. Haven't had a chance to get reacquainted with the neighbors. It may be an entirely new family that lives there. No one on The Row owns their home, after all. We all rent them."

"Well, it seems you have another murder to investigate, Pen," Benny said with a grin.

"Who the devil cares about that bloody body!" Mona screeched. "I'm set to be in an American prison. When father hears about this—"

"It'll be fine," Penelope tried to reassure her. "I...I think I can get us out of this."

"Yes! You could grease a few palms. Heaven knows you have enough kale for it," Ducky offered.

"I'd rather not risk adding a bribery charge to all of this. No, I know someone who can help."

Though, Pen did wonder if he would ever forgive her for this.

CHAPTER THREE

Back in the relative calm of the police station, especially in the quieter wee hours of the morning, Pen was able to charm her way into being allowed a phone call, one she assured the officers would help clear everything up.

To be fair, one look at their fine, but very wet clothes and the inability of a few of her cohorts to disguise their pretentious airs, and the officers knew they were dealing with folks who might cause the sort of headaches they didn't need at three o'clock in the morning.

All the same, they had shuffled the men off into a cell, much to Benny's experiential delight. Walter handled it with dull resignation. For all his talk of being an adventurer, Derrick put up quite the panicked ruckus as the bars were slammed on him.

Mona was so hysterical, they had taken her into an office to settle her down with a cup of coffee. Pen sat on a bench to await the arrival of her savior. He hadn't been happy when she called, his voice still groggy with sleep.

But when he entered through the front doors of the

station, he looked as handsome as Penelope had last remembered. He took a moment to close and shake his umbrella, then he approached the front desk, showing his badge.

"I'm Detective Richard Prescott. I was called on behalf of a Miss Penelope Banks?"

The desk sergeant simply pointed in her general direction behind him.

Detective Prescott's dark eyes, framed by enviable lashes that made her heart stutter a beat searched past him to seek her out. The burn scar, a remnant of the Great War, that ran from just beneath his right ear down his neck was barely noticeable when he finally faced her, an appropriate look of exasperation on his face. He removed his hat as he approached. He smoothed back his dark hair with his free hand.

Penelope mentally assessed the state of herself by comparison. She gingerly touched her dark hair, which had lost any hint of the waves she'd pinned last night. Each wet, limp strand clung to her scalp and the sides of her face, giving her horrid thoughts about what a picture she must present. At least the dark red dress with black beading she'd chosen for the party was still gorgeous and clung to her in a way that wasn't entirely terrible.

"Detective," the first officer said, walking over to greet him. "Care to tell me what it was that this one and her friends were doing breaking into the Washington Square Arch at this hour? Frankly, it's the kind of prank we expect from the kids going to that college or, more likely, those damn bohemian artist types. But this group seems more high-class than that."

"Looks can be very deceiving," he said tersely, meeting Pen with the kind of look she was used to from her father.

Still, she could see the subtle hint of begrudging amusement his eyes always carried when they fell on her.

He turned to the officer who had arrested them. "Tell me, was there any damage to person or property?"

"Well, no, but we did nab this one with a bottle of what we now know is gin in her hands," he jutted his chin toward Penelope.

Pen didn't have to guess how they were so certain. They'd probably have themselves a fine little party with it after she left the station.

Detective Prescott turned to flash a look of annoyance her way, as though she had just made his job that much harder.

"That bottle is quite old, I should point out," Pen protested. "My friend Derrick has just returned from many years abroad and happened to still have it in his home from the pre-Prohibition days, so it isn't bootleg."

She could tell from the ever so subtle gleam in his eye that Detective Prescott knew she was presenting the matter in a deliberately deceptive manner. Or really just outright lying.

Best to change the subject.

"However, there is the far more important matter of a dead body."

Both the officer and Detective Prescott looked at her with brows lifted for entirely different reasons—one in exasperation, the other in surprise.

"A dead body?"

"Yes, the woman I told you was by the fountain."

"We found no dead body at the scene," the officer insisted, sounding understandably defensive. "I should point out that no one else in her party saw a body, and...

well, she was quite under the influence by the time we got there. On a complaint for public disturbance, I should point out."

"Oh really now, lightning and thunder were causing more of a disturbance than we were."

"They were also going by animal names. This one was Pony."

"Pony?" Detective Prescott arched an eyebrow her way. She could see him biting back a smile.

"Now, you're deliberately muddling the point, officer," Penelope groused.

"Drinking in this day and age is a very serious crime, young lady," he huffed.

"I understand that officer, and like you, I'm perfectly appalled at how Prohibition has caused crime to run rampant in this city, giving dangerous criminals license to commit all manner of vicious deeds." The officer wrinkled his brow in confusion at the way Penelope had corrupted his intent. "But, really, do I seem like the sort of woman to associate with such unscrupulously violent criminals? As you stated earlier, this was nothing more than a prank, and one with no real victim. Surely something that warrants a fine, or perhaps even a sizable donation to some Policeman's organization?"

Detective Prescott shot her a wry smile.

The officer pursed his lips and narrowed his eyes. "If you're trying to offer a bribe, then—"

"I'm sure that's not at all what she meant, officer. She knows as well as I that you aren't susceptible to that sort of corruption. It's good men like you that keep the force working efficiently and ethically, maintaining the public's trust. I'll be sure to put in a good word with your sergeant— at a more decent hour of the morning, of course."

Penelope certainly hadn't meant anything criminal or unethical by the suggestion. But if it meant getting back to her warm apartment, a hot bath, and dry bed, she wouldn't have been opposed to it. Mona was right, this was no longer fun.

How had she been cajoled into doing something so ridiculous in the first place? It was Ducky, of course. His years in Europe had done nothing to temper his mischievous nature. Still, at the very least Wooly—*Walter* should have reined him in. He'd always been the level-headed best friend. Benny, of course, was game for anything. Pen still didn't know Mona that well, but she didn't seem like much of a risk-taker if her red, splotchy face, still streaked with tears was any indication.

"Obviously this crew of miscreants has to face some type of punishment," Detective Prescott said, rubbing his chin in thought.

Penelope felt herself get rankled, but knew better than to interject or object. She was quite familiar with his cunning ways of handling things. She was also quite familiar with how her meddlesome nature could get her into even more trouble than she already was.

"I'd hate to waste the court's time on this, turning it into the sort of spectacle that would draw headlines making a mockery of the police. Such publicity might also encourage all those nearby university students and bohemian artists to pull the same prank and waste even more police resources. No, I think it's in everyone's best interest to keep this one quiet. No need to turn them into anarchist heroes, wouldn't you say?"

Penelope bit back a grin, realizing what he was doing.

The officer seemed to be considering everything he said,

realizing the headache that might ensue if he decided to be hard-nosed about this.

"So what do you suggest?"

"I think a few citations with very hefty fines might teach them a good lesson. They seem like the type who hate losing money, especially over their own foolishness. I'm sure they, and more importantly, their influential families would be very grateful for that kind of leniency."

The officer didn't need to have that subtle threat explained to him. The area around Washington Square Park, particularly to the north, was fairly upper crust. And while New York University was more libertine than many of the other universities, there were still plenty of students in attendance who had influential families. Honestly, the same could be said of at least a few members of the bohemian artist set.

"If it helps, I can promise it won't happen again. We were just celebrating. Our friend, Ducky—*Derrick* has returned from a long period away. We're officially done celebrating—obviously. We're not career criminals. I mean, you saw poor Mona, does she seem like the nefarious sort?"

As though on cue, they heard Mona burst out into tears somewhere in the back office yet again. Pen was pleased to see how uncomfortable it made both men. All the more likely they'd want all of them gone from the station.

"Fine, fine," the officer grumbled.

Thirty minutes later, while Detective Prescott was still chatting in a back office with the head sergeant on duty at that hour, Derrick, Benny, Walter, and Mona were all carted off in various taxis and cars back to their respective abodes. Each of them had citations and fines that would have made the average person balk. But they all came from a financial set that easily spent the same amount on a dress or a nice suit without thinking twice.

Still, no need to rub anyone's nose in it.

Penelope had stayed behind to wait on Detective Prescott. When he was finally done with the sergeant, he approached her.

"I just wanted to thank you for your help, Detective Prescott," she said demurely.

He wasn't fooled by her show. "Shall I escort you home, Miss Banks? I'd hate for you to stumble into another bit of trouble tonight."

She pressed her lips together to keep from retorting something right back, at least while they were still in the station. She instead stood and took his offered arm. They walked out and he opened the large umbrella he'd brought with him, big enough to shield them both from the rain which was still coming down, though not as viciously as before.

Penelope moved in closer to him under the guise of getting more coverage from the umbrella. She liked the way his arm felt. Even under his coat and suit, she could feel how strong he was. From this standpoint, she had a full view of his scar running down into the collar of his shirt. It did nothing to lessen his appeal, and in fact, made her strangely more attracted to him.

"When I gave you my personal phone number, I didn't expect you to abuse it in such a manner, Miss Banks. Or should I call you Pony?" he said with a grin.

"It was either that or Piggy. I think I made the better choice. Of course, you could always call me Penelope?"

"I think, considering the hour we should keep it strictly professional. I'd hate for anyone to get the wrong idea."

"And what idea would that be?"

"That I've come here for any other reason beyond a simple courtesy."

"You mean you don't want to take advantage of the kindness you've shown me and ask for favors in return?"

"Now I'm wondering who would be the one taking advantage," he said, studying her with suspicion.

Penelope grinned. "If it makes you feel better, I didn't call you just to get me out of a pickle, detective. I would never abuse your considerate nature that way. Heaven help me if I can't spend a night in a jail cell. No, I called you because time is of the essence."

"Well, I was set to wake up a mere three hours from now anyway."

Penelope ignored his dry tone and continued. "It's the body I saw."

"The body no one else saw?"

"But that's what makes it all the more sinister!"

"I'm inclined to think it makes it decidedly less sinister. Either the body was never there, or the woman wasn't dead and simply came to and went on her merry way."

"No," Pen said shaking her head with insistence. "The condition she was in, she wouldn't be on her merry way anywhere. It was—"

Penelope took a moment to reimagine the scene in her head. The way her mind worked, even in just that brief flash of lightning, she could recall with perfect clarity what she'd seen.

"The stain on her dress! It was on her chest area, slightly darker than the surrounding material. I'm sure that's where she was stabbed or shot. Even if she was still alive, she was in no condition to get up and wander away on her own. I'm certain she was dead."

Detective Prescott considered her for a moment. Penelope knew him to be a reasonable man, who took his job seriously. She would have also liked to think they had worked together enough that he trusted her judgment.

Blessedly, he nodded. "Okay, let's go back and try and find out what happened to your mystery woman."

CHAPTER FOUR

It was still in the wee hours of the morning by the time the taxi drove through the arch of Washington Square Park along the road that ran through the park. Penelope had the driver drop Detective Prescott and her off near the fountain.

The rain had finally settled into a soft mist, which caused the light from the lamps to cast an eerie glow on the scene. Now that the rain was no longer pelting them, the unseemly types and the vagrants who were fearless or desperate enough to loiter in such public places were creeping back.

Pen was glad she was with Detective Prescott, who cut an imposing enough figure. Particularly when they made their way to the far side of the fountain where the lamp wasn't working.

"I didn't bring a flashlight with me. Though, I doubt we'd find anything here, not after that rain we just had."

He was right. Not only was it impossible to see anything in this part of the park while it was still dark, but the heavy rain would have washed away any evidence.

The person who had killed her, whoever she was, had certainly gotten lucky with the weather.

But why come to take her body away after the fact?

"We need to question the people in that house," Penelope said, pointing to the townhouse along The Row she'd noted earlier. The lights were still out. "I saw her fighting with someone in that house earlier, someone who got physical with her."

"You want me to wake them at this hour of the morning?"

"Need I remind you this is a potential murder? If we had a body, you'd have no qualms about knocking on their door."

"Because I'd have bona fide proof of a crime."

"My word isn't good enough? After all we've been through together?"

"I trust you think you saw something, Miss Banks. But it isn't you that I have to answer to. I go knocking on people's doors this hour of the morning over a crime that no one else saw happen, particularly after helping the only witness—with whom too many people know I have a history—wriggle her way out of jail time, and my lieutenant is going to have words with me, more importantly, he'll have words with *his* boss about me."

"And if you end up solving a murder, or better yet saving a woman's life? She could be back in that house this very moment in the clutches of the person who attacked her."

He stared at her and she could feel that same exasperation set in. Thankfully, his civic-mindedness ruled the day.

"I suppose you have a point," he said in resignation.

"Thank you, detective."

They walked over together, still huddled underneath the umbrella even though it was still only misting.

The Row, located along Washington Square North was a famously desirable part of the city. The red brick facade with white marble trim harkened back to the Greek Revival of the Georgian era in which they had first been built in the 1830s. Greenwich Village, in which it was located had been an artist's paradise for well over a decade. Thus, the rest of the neighborhood had begun shifting from tenement housing or factories to nicer apartment buildings.

But that didn't mean murder couldn't have still happened there.

Detective Prescott rang the electrified bell to announce them. It took a long time, several minutes in fact, for them to see a light come on. The man who came to the door was wise enough to look at them through the side window instead of opening the door, considering the hour.

Detective Prescott flashed his badge, which did nothing to erase the disgruntled look on the man's face. He sighed and released the curtain. A moment later the door opened for them.

He was in his early thirties with thinning strawberry blond hair, more blond than strawberry, and pale blue eyes. He tightened the dark blue quilted robe with satin trim firmly around him.

"What's the meaning of this? Do you have any idea what time it is?"

"I'm Detective Prescott, and I apologize for the time, Mr...?"

"Whitley, William Whitley," he snapped. "Now, what is this about?"

"There has been a report of a body near the fountain in

the park, and we were wondering if perhaps the victim was a resident or guest of this house."

"This home?" he asked, more outraged than horrified. "A woman you say? What did she look like?"

Penelope answered. "Red hair, dressed in a dark blue, silver-beaded dress with silver heels."

He narrowed his eyes at Penelope. "You must be mistaken. No one with that description resides here."

"Perhaps a guest?"

He gave her an impatient look. "There is *no one* under this roof who matches that description."

"It's just that I saw her earlier through the window. It was about two hours ago?"

"Do you mean to tell me you were snooping into our windows in the middle of the night?"

"No, I was...nearby," Penelope said, trying not to sound too defensive.

"In the middle of the rain?" He turned to Detective Prescott. "Perhaps an insane asylum would be more appropriate for her than leading her around to the homes of people whose privacy she has no problem invading. A woman who idles in public parks at obscene hours of the night is surely up to no good."

"Perhaps you should answer the question, Mr. Whitley," Detective Prescott said in a curt voice. "Are you saying that a woman with red hair, dressed in that manner has not been in this house tonight?"

"I've been here all night, and there was no such woman."

"Perhaps one of the other members of the household—"

"Are all still firmly asleep, despite this rude intrusion at an indecent hour." He narrowed his eyes. "And before you ask, no I will not wake them for this nonsense. You can come back at a more decent hour after breakfast if you need to speak with them."

"We need to search the home," Penelope pleaded with Detective Prescott. "She could be in there right now."

"You most certainly will not!" William Whitley snapped. "You do *not* have my permission to do such a thing, and you have no cause, never mind a warrant. The word of a lunatic woman is certainly not enough reason for you to barrel your way in past me. Now, if there's nothing more?"

Detective Prescott sighed. "No, but I will be back later in the morning to talk with the rest of your family."

"I'm sure they'll be waiting with bells on, detective, until then..." He shut the door on them. One moment later the light he'd turned on went dark.

"Is that it?" Penelope cried in frustration.

"He was right, there isn't much I can do based solely on your word, Miss Banks."

"Oh for heaven's sake, can't you just say Penelope or Pen. You always make me feel like such a bluenose when you call me Miss Banks."

"Will Pony suffice?" He said with a half grin.

It was enough to diffuse her frustration and, despite the macabre circumstances, breathe out a laugh.

He led them down the few steps to the sidewalk.

"So, what do you think?" Penelope asked, wondering if the denial of William Whitley was enough to dissuade him from following through on this.

"I think," he began, then exhaled, "that he is definitely hiding something."

"You do?"

"I do. Most people would be filled with concern, or at least alarmed curiosity if a detective came to their door at this hour of the night. Has someone they loved either been hurt or killed? Gotten themselves into trouble? He only seemed irate, which was understandable, but without a hint of anything else. It almost felt like he was expecting this and had already built up his defenses ahead of time."

"So you think he killed her?" Penelope asked, instinctively grabbing his arm more firmly underneath their umbrella.

"I wouldn't leap to that conclusion just yet, but I do think it's worth taking a closer look."

"I knew it!"

"I suppose it's pointless to tell you I'll be back to question them on my own, *without* the aid of any civilians?"

"I understand, detective. Or may I say Richard?"

He chose to focus on her instant agreement to not meddle rather than the question about his name. "Is this you actually listening for once when I say not to do something that should be left to the police?"

"Yes, but I should point out that it is every civilian's right to enjoy the park on a fine day after a bit of rain, is it not?"

"I should have known there'd be a catch."

"No catch, just a little enjoyment of one of the attractions this fair city of ours has to offer."

"I suppose there's nothing I can do or say to dissuade you?"

"Would you really deny me a day in the park? Perhaps I'll make a picnic of it."

"And just when I was getting used to calling you Penelope."

"Don't be like that, Richard."

"Detective Prescott."

"So formal again?"

"I have a feeling I may have to get you out of another pickle in the near future, one where being too familiar would be problematic for us both."

"Or you could invite me to dinner like a proper gentleman."

"If only you behaved like a proper lady."

"No need to be insulting."

He grinned. "That was hardly an insult, and something tells me you wouldn't see it as one."

She laughed. "See? You already know me so well, Richard."

"Detective Prescott."

"*Detective.* I suppose I shall see you in passing in the park."

"I would say I look forward to it, but something tells me I may regret it."

CHAPTER FIVE

THE NEXT MORNING, PENELOPE WAS UP EARLY AND surprisingly spry considering her adventurous night and only four hours of sleep. She was eager to get back to Washington Square Park now that the light of day had come. Last night's rain was long gone, leaving plenty of sun with which to observe the Whitley house from afar.

She dressed herself rather than wait for the fuss of their new maid, Emma, to help her. Pen had taken a long luxurious bath as soon as she'd returned home last night so she just splashed herself with a bit of lavender water and put on a simple twill frock.

Perfect for a picnic in the park.

Washington Square was usually filled with an odd mix of bohemian artists, university students, and mothers or nannies with babies and children, so she didn't want to stand out too much while she was there.

Chives, her butler, was of course already up. Professional that he was, he gave no hint that he was well aware she had crept into her 5th Avenue apartment well after decent society was safely ensconced in their beds.

"Good morning, Miss Banks."

"Good morning, Chives. Has Arabella started cooking breakfast yet?"

"She has, did you have a special request?"

"No, I'll just pop in, I so rarely get to see her."

"I'm sure she would like that," he said in a tactful way, though he probably abhorred the idea. Still, Agnes, his old employer had never been one for societal norms either.

Arabella was singing away, an aria in the wrong note, as she scrambled eggs.

"Good morning, Arabella."

"Aye!" She jumped in surprise and spun around with her hand to her chest. "Saints alive, Miss Penelope. You're enough to give a woman a heart attack, aren't you just?"

"I'm sorry, I didn't mean to scare you," Penelope said, feeling bad.

"Nonsense, nonsense, child." It seemed Arabella would always think of Pen as that precocious child who enjoyed wandering around Agnes's mansion. Pen didn't mind. Even her habit of calling her Miss Penelope instead of Miss Banks seemed rather endearing. "It's always lovely to see you of course. What with this job of yours, I hardly ever get a chance, do I?"

"I'll have to make it a point to visit more."

"What can I do for you? Did you want something special for breakfast?"

"No, but I would like something special for the day. I plan on having a picnic."

"Oh, how lovely. But it rained something awful last night, didn't it just? I can't imagine how enjoyable that would be."

Pen winked. "One of the hazards of my job. I'm on a spy mission."

"Oh, heavens! How exciting! But you won't go getting yourself into any danger, will you Miss Penelope?"

"Perish the thought. Still, it's probably wise that Cousin Cordelia doesn't find out. You know how her nerves are."

Arabella nodded with overt sympathy. "Yes, the poor woman does take so much to heart, bless her. What is it you'd like for this picnic?"

"Just a few sandwiches will do. Nothing special."

"You leave it to Arabella. As soon as I've finished breakfast, I'll have something made up for you quick as a whip, won't I?"

"Bless you, Arabella."

Penelope made her way into the library, where Cousin Cordelia and she usually ate. The cozy ambiance and the lovely view of Central Park made it a much more enjoyable spot to dine than the grand dining room.

She had to pass through the living room, where Lady Dinah, a white Persian cat she'd adopted from a recent case, and her three rapidly growing kittens, who had yet to be named, were already up and at it. Lady Di was lounging on an armchair, completely indifferent to the chaos her children were creating underneath the side table. Pen smiled at them but quickly continued before the all-orange kitten noticed her and bounded over. For some reason, he in particular seemed to like fussing with Penelope's legs, destroying her stockings. She was thinking of calling him Little Monster if they couldn't find a home for them soon.

Pen sat down at the table and stared out the window, enjoying a cup of coffee Chives magically made appear as she waited for Cousin Cordelia to join her. She was the first cousin of Penelope's father and had taken Pen in when he had cut her off three years ago. Now that Pen was flush with more kale than she needed, she had returned the favor.

"Ah, Penelope, you're up."

She turned at the sound of her cousin's voice as she entered. However, her attention was caught by Emma trailing her, a handkerchief to her eyes.

"Are you all right, Emma?" Penelope asked with concern.

"I'm so sorry, Miss." Emma sniffed and snatched the handkerchief away, holding it behind her back as she straightened up. "I'm fine."

"Apparently not."

"Poor dear, she found out last night that her beloved aunt died," Cousin Cordelia said as she sat down with Penelope.

"My mother's aunt, actually. Haven't seen her since I was a little girl. She lives in Michigan. To think, she was all alone when the end came. She and my mother didn't see eye to eye, but that never stopped her from being kind to me and my sister. She was always so generous at Christmas and birthdays."

"Well, if you need time off to go to the funeral or handle any affairs, we of course understand."

"Thank you, miss, but that won't be necessary. I apologize for ruining your morning."

"You're hardly the worst thing that's happened this morning, Emma."

She flashed a smile. "I'll go see about breakfast."

When she was gone Cousin Cordelia couldn't help herself. "Such an emotional young thing. Apparently, she was six the last time she saw her in person. I'm not sure why there's so much fuss."

"There was obviously still affection there. Maybe they kept in touch via letters?"

"Perhaps. Speaking of old connections how was your little reunion last night with Derrick Bishop?"

Pen had absolutely no intention of telling her cousin about being arrested or what led up to it. That would have her calling for her "medicine," really just bootleg brandy, being that her prescription had run out years ago.

"It was...boisterous."

"Oh, I hope you didn't get too wild, I know how you young people are."

"Mostly just catching up with one another."

"He must be so cultured, all that time spent in Europe, visiting museums and attending operas. They really are quite sophisticated over there aren't they?"

Pen had to bite back a smile at the thought of Ducky whiling his time away doing anything so refined.

"Ducky is still...Ducky."

"Ducky, what a silly name. Hopefully, this fiancée of his puts an end to that nonsense. What is she like?"

"Mona? She's pretty of course. Half-British."

"Oh!" Cousin Cordelia exclaimed with glee, fervent anglophile that she was. "You must invite them to dinner. Honestly, considering how often your mother entertained—not that I necessarily approved of all her invitees—I'm surprised you haven't yet. It's such a lovely apartment Agnes left you."

"It's something to consider. In the meantime, I have a rather interesting day at work. A new case has landed in my lap. Don't worry, I won't give you the details, I know how much you abhor that, Cousin."

"Thank you dear, you know how such things try my nerves." Her cousin sipped her coffee but eyed Pen over the rim. After swallowing, she set it back down. "Perhaps just a hint won't be too upsetting, nothing *too* descriptive."

Pen held back a smile. "A murder."

"Oh!"

"Should I stop?" Penelope asked with overt concern.

"Please do."

"Of course."

Breakfast was brought out and just as Pen picked up her fork, her cousin spoke again.

"It wasn't...horrid was it?"

"Nothing grotesque. I found her lying in Washington Square Park near the fountain, stabbed or shot."

"Dear me! What *is* this city coming to? Women being ravished and left for dead in public parks. Wild, vicious men doing heaven knows what while we sleep. Not even safe in our own homes. I knew nothing good would come from those automobiles racing around everywhere."

Pen couldn't help a small laugh. "My, my, Cousin, I dare say you may have figured out the case for me! And all without any such illuminating details on my part."

"Well, one never knows."

"I have a feeling it was a family squabble."

"I still say society has gone to the wolves. I suspect I shall need an extra dose of medicine today."

"Naturally, just try not to overdose on it. I'd hate to lose you. Someone might suspect me of doing you in!"

"Really Penelope, how you do like to exaggerate things."

"Wherever do I get it from?"

CHAPTER SIX

"WE'RE GOING ON A PICNIC, JANE!" PENELOPE announced as soon as she entered the office of her private investigation business.

"A picnic?" Jane Pugley, her associate asked, her pale, cornflower blue eyes understandably bewildered. She tucked back a strand of her light brown hair, still old-fashionably long, but done up in a pretty, loose chignon. "Is there a special occasion?"

"Well, it's a fine day, don't you think?" Penelope replied, her own much brighter blue eyes wide with enthusiasm.

"Yes, but it rained something awful last night."

"Which is why I brought extra blankets for us to sit on."

"Are you worried about the lack of business? I'm sure it will pick up soon, Miss Banks." Penelope had long since given up asking her to call her Pen, as her friends did, or even Penelope.

"Okay, I confess, we have a new case to solve."

"We do?" Jane said, brightening up.

"Yes, a case, which just so happens to be centered in

41

Washington Square. So, up, up! Arabella has packed us some delicious sandwiches, peaches, and almond cake with which we can while away the day. Leonard has the car running, ready to whisk us downtown. Come, come!"

On the way down to Washington Square Park, Penelope plied Jane with the details of last night's events. She had no fear of revealing her *technically* illegal bit of mischief, being that Leonard, her chauffeur, was already used to her various misadventures and had yet to judge her, and Jane was far too tactful to admonish her.

"My, what an...adventure that must have been," Jane said hesitantly.

"I know, I know, it was all perfectly illegal, but a victimless crime all the same." Penelope waved it off. "Besides, if it wasn't for that little act of criminality I never would have seen the body of this poor woman, who everyone is perfectly happy to believe never even existed!"

"And you're certain you saw her?"

"I am," Penelope said twisting the side of her mouth with irritation at yet another proclamation of doubt.

"I don't believe you *didn't* see her, Miss Banks, I just... how did she disappear?"

"That's what I plan on finding out." She leaned in to address Leonard. "Be a dear, and go around to the east side of the park and drop us off there."

Penelope wanted to make sure they wouldn't be seen exiting the car, just in case any of the Whitleys were peeking through curtains with suspicion. She wasn't sure if any of them beyond William Whitley had seen her last night, and she didn't want to be found out before she'd even begun spying on them. She carried the hamper that Arabella had conjured up from somewhere, while Jane carried the folded blankets for them to sit on.

It was already ten in the morning on a pleasant and sunny day. Thus, the park was beginning to fill with the usual sorts. Pen could easily identify them all. On the other side of the road that ran through the middle of the park, the children were running around or playing near the fountain under the watchful eyes of their mothers or governesses. They were well separated from the artists and students lounging about, smoking, playing instruments, drawing and painting, or arguing and laughing amongst themselves.

Penelope picked a patch of grass on the east side, almost near the playground. It was well hidden by trees, but one could still observe every window of her particular home of interest on The Row.

"Now then, this seems like the perfect place to set up."

They both realized how incorrect that assessment was as soon as they stepped foot on the grass. Pen's small heel sank right into the soggy soil. It was no wonder they were the only ones with the bright idea of having a picnic on such a pleasant day.

"Soldier on, Jane. I'll pay for new shoes if yours get ruined. Sometimes detective work is messy."

Jane, bless her, didn't complain. Pen took hold of the first blanket, stuffing it under her free arm while Jane unfurled the other to set on the still wet grass. She took the other from Pen and laid it on top of that.

"There now, safe and dry," she said in a chipper tone.

Jane flashed an uncertain smile.

They both instinctively kept their muddy heels hanging over the edge as they settled down.

While Jane unpacked the food for the day, Penelope's eyes wandered to the far side of the fountain where four young men had just settled down.

How had the dead woman ended up on that side of the

fountain specifically? It was too exposed to assume her murderer had been trying to hide her body. On the other hand, it had been dark on that side, so perhaps they hadn't meant for her to be easily seen, at least not until morning. Maybe it was all mere coincidence?

But then why remove her again?

"Are these opera glasses?" Jane asked, drawing Pen's attention.

"Yes, the perfect tool for a little spying. Heaven knows that's what most opera attendees use them for, at least those seated in the boxes. That devilish little device is strong enough to identify a single Swarovski crystal missing from a gown."

"I see," Jane said, the look on her face indicating she didn't see at all. One of these days, Penelope would have to take her to the opera to get the full experience.

Penelope took hold of them and brought them up to her eyes, swiveling around to face the townhome she was focused on. All the curtains were still drawn at the Whitley residence, even though it was well past ten in the morning by now. She sighed and pulled them away.

"What is it we're looking for, Miss Banks?"

"I want to keep an eye on that home, and anyone who may exit it. We need to learn as much as we can about that Whitley family."

Penelope was under no impression that they would be daft enough to carry out a body, perhaps rolled up in a rug or stuffed into a trunk, in broad daylight. Especially after getting a visit from a detective and a witness. Still, perhaps spending the day observing them might glean something about what might have happened last night.

After a mere twenty minutes of no activity, Penelope became restless. She didn't realize just how dull espionage could be. Next to her, even Jane sighed with boredom as she finished a peach.

"I'm going to explore the fountain," Pen announced, jumping up from the blankets.

"Aren't you worried about being seen?"

"The park is filled with people now. No one will notice me, especially with this sunhat on." Pen had worn it specifically, in the hopes that the brim would help mask her face.

She casually strolled the walkway until she got to the road that ran right through the park. Pen loved cars as much as any modern young woman, though she had yet to learn how to drive. Still, it seemed a shame to have a park essentially cut in half by such an obnoxious nuisance. One day perhaps they'd build a pedestrian bridge to the other side, or just close the road altogether and force drivers to go around the park.

When there was a break in traffic she flitted across toward the fountain. Penelope made her way to the southwest side where she had seen the woman sprawled on the ground. Unfortunately, there was the irksome presence of the four animated young men she had seen arrive earlier. She stood back a ways to try and observe the scene hoping she would find something to help her make sense of it all, but found it hard to concentrate over their loud debate. The men obviously attended NYU law school, being that they were arguing over some upcoming criminal case down in Tennessee concerning a teacher who had taught something illegal.

"He was essentially calling the Bible a load of bunk, that we all come from monkeys."

"He didn't teach that, Cal, he simply offered the well-accepted *theory* that perhaps we evolved, and no not from monkeys but from—"

"It wouldn't surprise me to find out that you and yours came from swinging monkeys, Alfie. *Hooo, hoo, hee hee!*"

"Brilliant argument, Georgie. I can only imagine what an invaluable contribution you'll make to the legal profession."

"Alfie has a point, Cal, why not teach both evolution and creation and let people decide?"

"Thank you, Thomas."

"Keep it out of schools, I say, at least at that age. Now, in universities—"

"Or some communist commune!"

"Let me finish, George. Ultimately, that Scopes fella broke Tennessee law and that's that. I'm pretty sure the trial in a few weeks will confirm it."

"The ACLU thinks maybe—"

"Ha, ha, speaking of communists!"

"Gentlemen, gentlemen, let's look at it from an academic point of view. Should the law even have been..."

God save us from pontificators! Penelope groused in her head.

Who cared about evolution or what was being taught in Tennessee classrooms? Though, if what they were saying was true, Pen did have a bit of respect for a teacher who so boldly flouted societal dictates. Why not let students decide if they believed in creation or evolution? All the same, she needed to focus on the woman who had died last night.

"Here's a gal who seems to have an opinion. Say, sweetheart, what do you think about teaching kids that we all come from talking apes?"

"Oh leave her alone, Georgie, she obviously has something else on her mind."

Penelope wrinkled her brow with annoyance that they

had finally noticed her. She had been perfectly fine ignoring them in the hopes they'd do the same.

"Hey, I think she's pondering it," said the one named Cal with a grin. He had dark hair and intense, dark eyes giving him a devilishly handsome appearance. "How can anyone look at this vision of delight and think we come from monkeys?"

Penelope narrowed her eyes, considering the four in a new light. "You all go to the law school?"

"How'd you guess?"

Penelope ignored that sardonic question and continued. "Have you studied criminal law yet?"

"It's a requirement for first year, but we've just graduated. We're *supposed* to be studying for the bar right now," said the one named Thomas—curly brown hair, strenuously combed into waves—giving them all reproachful looks. "But of course, criminal law is a part of the exam."

"Perfect, let me pose a question to you. Let's say you killed a woman in the middle of the night, perhaps in one of the buildings surrounding this park." Penelope idly waved a hand toward The Row, hoping it didn't seem deliberate. "One of those homes for example. Why would you then bring the body all the way to the fountain, specifically here on this side?"

They all stared at her, completely silent, each with various expressions ranging from perfectly shocked to perfectly wary.

"It's purely academic, of course," she assured them, though it didn't seem to assure them at all.

"Is this some kind of joke?" Thomas asked.

"This gal's obviously missing the gravy off her pork chops."

"No, no, Calvin," said Georgie, or perhaps it was just

George. He hopped up from his perch and approached her, hands in his pockets. "Let's work this out. After all, we're soon to be learned men of the law ourselves."

"Okay, why'd you kill her?" Alfred, the tall one with glasses asked.

"That's irrelevant."

"It's never irrelevant. In fact, it may very well explain why you brought her here."

Pen thought about it. "That's a good point. Let's say I don't know."

"You don't know why you killed her?"

"Pretend I'm the detective trying to figure it out. What would you learned men of the law say?"

"Obviously they wanted the body to be found."

"No," Penelope said, twisting her mouth with frustration. "Last night this side of the fountain was in pure darkness. That light up there was out."

"Hey, I thought you said this was academic!" Thomas protested.

"Okay, not academic. How about...investigative?"

"Is this body real or not, doll?" Calvin asked

"*That's* irrelevant."

"I think we'd better get back to studying," he said, eyeing Pen with an incredulous stare as he puffed a cigarette.

"I'm curious though," Alfred said.

"Me too," Georgie, the blond one with an attractively dimpled smile, quickly concurred, giving Pen a flirtatious grin. He held out his hand. "George Hamilton, no relation to the founding father," he added with a wink. "You can call me Georgie."

"I'm staying too," Thomas said. "Anything to avoid the torture of reviewing Property Law."

"So *was* there a body here?" Alfred asked, getting back on topic as Penelope distractedly shook Georgie's hand.

"There was, last night, around two in the morning."

"It was pouring rain then!" Georgie said.

"Exactly, all the more reason it's strange, no?"

"Well, not exactly," Alfred said, pushing his glasses higher up his nose. He squinted and slowly spun around, looking at the buildings, then turned back to her. "In fact, the rain would have made a perfect cover, the moon would be blocked by the clouds and I doubt too many people were up and about then."

"There, you have your reason why!" Georgie announced. "Now then, doll, let's say you and I go—"

"Still, wouldn't it make sense to take the body to the trees, where you could be certain no one would see you?" Pen said, ignoring him in favor of Alfie.

Cal and Thomas chuckled. Penelope gave them a questioning look. The latter answered first.

"We all live in this part of town. Calvin and I each have an apartment in that building over there," Thomas said, pointing to what looked like a moderately renovated tenement building to the west of the park. "You obviously don't know what this neighborhood is like that time of night, especially the further south you go. The trees would be crawling with tramps and vagrants. They'd have sheltered under them during the rain. They know they'd be shooed away, or worse, arrested if they tried to seek shelter under any awnings or in doorways."

"So that suggests the murderer wanted the body to be hidden and chose the option safest for them?" Penelope asked Alfred, who she realized was the one most likely to help her. "But why drag her all the way here? It's the middle of the park."

"Exactly, equal distance from any building surrounding it."

Penelope slowly spun around like he did, realizing he was right. "So no one would tie the body to a specific building, or even a particular street."

"Huzzah! So, do we get a prize?" Cal said with a sardonic smile.

Pen ignored him again in favor of Alfred. "So you drag the body all the way out here. What would make you then move it again?"

"Is that what happened?" Thomas asked with a puzzled look.

Penelope nodded.

"And I assume you didn't see who took it?" Georgie asked.

"No, by the time we got down, she was already gone."

"Down from what?"

"Never mind that," Pen said quickly.

She focused her attention on Alfred who seemed to be considering it. He pushed up his glasses, and Penelope realized that behind them were a lovely pair of green eyes. She observed him more thoroughly. He was tall, but not lanky or too hefty. It was mostly the glasses and his overly serious manner that made him go unnoticed on a quick pass by. In fact, he was rather handsome in a studious, inconspicuous sort of way.

Nothing compared to the dashing Detective Prescott of course.

"Well, the way I see it, either your reasons for leaving her here changed, or this had been a temporary stop on the way to where you were really taking her body."

Penelope considered that, reversing her mind back to last night. Something Alfie just said pricked something in her brain. She'd first seen the woman in a flash of lightning when the storm was at its worst. What had happened around that time?

"Of course!" she finally announced.

"You've figured it out?" Alfred asked with deep interest. The three others leaned in with equally avid curiosity.

"I think so, all thanks to you." Without thinking she pulled him in and planted a kiss on his cheek. "Thanks, Alfie, you're the berries!"

He seemed perfectly stunned, those green eyes blinking rapidly. Pen wasted no time trotting back toward Jane.

Behind her, she heard Georgie call out in protest. "Hey, wait a minute, where's my kiss? How about a name? At least tell us what you figured out! Was it the butler? It was the butler who did it, wasn't it?" He laughed at his own joke.

Pen laughed despite herself as she waited for another break in traffic to cross back to Jane.

"We're getting together again tonight, come with us and we can discuss another murder!" Georgie added.

Pen shook her head in disbelief, not turning back. He really was shameless. She could only wonder what the mothers and nannies around them were thinking. Obviously, Georgie was the bad boy of that quartet.

She focused her attention on the road. Across the way, she saw a man approaching a perfectly oblivious Jane as she sat with her opera glasses trained on the home Pen had told her to watch.

"Oh no!"

CHAPTER SEVEN

PENELOPE DARTED OUT INTO THE ROAD, IGNORING THE blare of a car horn as it just missed her. She hurried over to the blanket where Jane sat, wincing as her heels once again sunk into the grass.

"Oh no you don't!" she announced.

Benny Davenport spun around, his mouth pursed in mock offense. He was handsome in an effeminate sort of way, with full lips and an aquiline nose. His dark hair was combed straight back away from his high forehead, highlighting his patrician looks. "Whatever do you mean, Pen?"

"This is a very serious bit of work we're doing. I won't have you distracting us with silly gossip. You were bad enough last night."

"Nonsense, I was just strolling through the park and happened to notice dear Jane here. Thought I'd pop over to say hello."

"Oh really?"

"It seems rather odd to have a picnic today of all days and here of all places. I know for a fact that Pen is aware it rained quite heavily last night." He gave her a taunting look.

"Don't you find the ground a bit moist for such an adventure?"

Pen wrinkled her nose at that word. "This isn't a lark, we're here for work. Which means no lingering for you!"

Despite her protests, Benny fell right onto the blanket and grabbed a peach. He lay on his side and insolently took a bite, grinning at her from behind it.

"So, what is this 'work' you two doves are up to?"

Penelope sighed and sat down on the blanket.

"We're spying," Jane said in a gleefully conspiratorial voice. She enjoyed Benny, who did have his moments, when he wasn't being perfectly devilish.

"Of course you are," Benny said, arching an eyebrow Penelope's way. "Did our Pen happen to tell you what fun we had last night?"

"Everything," Jane said, her eyes darting to the arch. "I think I would have died going all the way up there. Whatever made you think of doing such a thing?"

Benny sat up with excitement. "Oh, now there's a story for you. You see back in 1917, a group of artists had the original bright idea of doing it—John Sloan, Marcel Duchamp." At Jane's blank expression he continued. "What about the poet, Gertrude Drick?"

Jane shook her head in complete ignorance and shrugged apologetically.

Benny patted her on the leg. "Not to worry, dove. Benny shall make an aesthete out of you eventually."

"A what?"

"Exactly," He said with a frown. "Anyway, continuing on. Why they chose January of all months is beyond me. They went all the way to the top for an impromptu little party. Despite the cold, it all seems like it was such good fun, they laid blankets, hung Chinese lanterns, tied red balloons to the arch, sipped tea, even shot off cap pistols."

"No!" Jane gasped, then laughed.

"That's not all," he continued, quickly turning back to lying on his side and arching an eyebrow. "At some point Gertrude declared all you see before you the Free and Independent Republic of Washington Square. Oh, if only! Just think what sort of fun could be had with no rules or restraints."

"Careful Benny, you're beginning to sound like one of those anarchists."

"I sometimes wonder if I'm not one at heart," he said forlornly, falling back onto the blanket in despair. "This is what comes from a life of imposed repression, Jane. I pity to think of what else we've missed out on in life."

"Yes, such poor unfortunate souls you and I are," Penelope said in a sarcastic tone.

"Exactly," Benny said without a hint of irony as he turned to lie on his side again and finish his peach.

"Don't pretend you were here at the park by coincidence, Benny."

"Of course not!" He laughed. "I know you far too well, Pen. I figured you'd be here doing your little investigation of this body you claim you saw last night."

"So you didn't see it, Benny?" Jane asked.

"I was too busy keeping Ducky from becoming a body himself. He nearly toppled over the edge and fell to his death!"

"No!" Jane exclaimed.

"Speaking of Ducky, I think he may very well be the reason why the body disappeared. I was talking to a group of young men who go to the law school—"

"Were they handsome?" Benny asked, eyes suddenly wide with interest.

Jane giggled nervously, still not quite used to Benny's "particularity."

"Never mind that! At any rate, one of them helped me recall exactly why the body may have been moved."

"Do tell."

"Well, I first saw her in the middle of the worst part of that thunderstorm. We could barely see our own hands before our eyes then, remember?"

"My hands were rather preoccupied if you recall."

"Yes, of course. But I happened to be looking over the edge at the time, and it was during a flash of lightning that I saw the body. But just before that Ducky was shouting at the top of his lungs. Do you remember what he said?"

"Some nonsense about Duckland."

"'I see you!' Pen said in exasperation. "That's what he said, loudly enough for anyone to hear."

Benny laughed. "And you think that's what caused the woman to walk off on her own?"

"No, Benny," Jane said, lightly slapping him on the shoulder. "But if you had just moved a body, those are the last words you'd want to hear someone shouting."

"I see my Dr. Watson is more than earning her keep, and she wasn't even there! Keen observation, Jane."

"Thank you, Miss Banks," Jane said, glowing.

"So you think the person who put the body there was spooked by Ducky's silly announcement and decided to remove it?"

"The ultimate evidence of their crime? Of course!"

"So where is the body now?"

Pen turned to the house where she'd first seen the

woman. "I think she's back in there, awaiting the perfect opportunity to be moved again."

"Unless they moved her after you were taken away to jail," Jane offered.

"Do you suppose the murderer was the one who called the police on us?" Benny asked.

"I doubt it. The last thing I'd want is the police conveniently on the scene if I had just moved a body back to my home and there were self-proclaimed witnesses about."

"But once we were conveniently gone, it gave them perfect opportunity to move it out of the house," Benny pointed out.

"Pineapples!" Penelope hissed in frustration.

"We really do have to introduce you to some more choice expletives, Pen. This is getting embarrassing."

"Perhaps you could be even more useful and tell me what you remember from last night. You saw the lights on in that home, didn't you? Did you notice anything through the windows?"

Benny seemed to be considering it in earnest. "Not really, but tell me what you remember."

"Well, they only came on just before I managed to pick the lock."

"Perhaps it was just a party?"

"What party gets started that late at night?"

Benny gave her a droll look.

"On *that* side of the park?"

"Why not? Ducky lives on The Row, only a few houses down. Speaking of which, why aren't you at his house interrogating him right now?"

"His parents are back from Newport by now. No need to inform them of what we were up to. Besides, I thought I'd give Mona at least the morning to recover. She didn't take too well to being arrested last night."

"So for now, you're just sitting and watching? Have you seen anything interesting yet? Anyone walking out with a large trunk?" He asked, waggling his eyebrows.

"No, it's been rather boring, in fact," Jane said.

"Perhaps I should liven things up by telling you the history of Washington Square," Benny said with a wicked grin. "Did you know that this was once a public hanging ground? Right after the Revolutionary War, they strung up all the traitors right here for all to see."

"Really?" Jane said, thrilled.

"That's why it's named Washington Square Park, where the first president vanquished his enemies! It serves as a warning to anyone who dares go against the United States."

"Don't start embellishing, Benny. That's not true," Pen admonished.

"I like my version," he scoffed, then an impish look came to his face. "But if you go back even further, this was once a potter's field."

"What's that?" Jane asked.

"A place where dead bodies were buried. Disease ran rife in this part of town which was nothing more than marshland. They simply threw the dead into large pits and were done with it. Didn't even bother removing them before building everything you see before you. Rumor has it that they kept finding bones as they built the fountain. They had to push them all into the grassy bits. We could be sitting on hundreds of dead bodies right now!"

"Really?" Jane squealed, darting her eyes back and forth to either side of the blanket in horror.

"Stop scaring her, Benny," Penelope said, though she

didn't deny this bit of history. Even she knew this much was true, having read it at some point out of morbid curiosity.

"With all this rain, it's certainly created conditions that might make them rise to the surface. Maybe that's where your body went, Pen. The dead rose up to reclaim one of theirs!"

"Stop it, now, Benny," Pen admonished, noting how white Jane had gone at that suggestion.

"I'm fine, Miss Banks. I know he's teasing," Jane said, though she did suddenly lose interest in her sandwich.

"Oh, I'm sorry, dove. I do get carried away," Benny said, patting her hand. "How about a gentler bit of history? This park was also where the first public telegraph was sent way back in…"

"1838," Penelope finished for him. "January the sixth."

"Of course, our Pen would remember the exact date."

"Our Pen is getting rather bored of history lessons. Perhaps it is a good thing you're here, Benny. Entertain us with some tawdry gossip instead. I swear that house appears to be as dead as the body I saw last night. Where is everyone?"

No sooner had she spoken those words than she saw a man who had been walking down the street carrying a bouquet of tulips suddenly turn to ascend the stairs of the Whitley residence.

"It seems we finally have a bit of activity," she said, grabbing the opera glasses to get a better look.

Through the glasses, she could only see the back of the man's hat, but she did see that the door was opened by a housemaid. She was shaking her head in response to something the man had asked.

"Oh, how I wish I was better at reading lips," she lamented.

When the door was closed, the man stood there for a few seconds, as though wondering what to do.

"It seems our suitor has been denied," Benny said.

"Poor thing," Jane commiserated.

Pen pulled her glasses away and hopped up from her sitting position.

"Where are you going?" Benny asked.

"Keep watch, you two. I plan on finding out who he is and what he wanted."

CHAPTER EIGHT

PENELOPE TOOK A SIDE PATH TO EXIT THE PARK SO SHE wouldn't be noticed as she approached the man leaving the Whitley home. The rejected suitor had just descended the stairs. She eased her pace, so it would seem as though she was also a resident of this neighborhood.

Pen studied him as she approached. He was wearing a very nice suit, expensive even. But a closer look by a trained eye would be enough to dissuade anyone from thinking that he had the kind of money that afforded him a residence on The Row. For one thing, it wasn't quite tailored to his form and was a few years out of fashion.

As Pen neared him, she noted that he was quite attractive. He had a longish face with a proud nose and full mouth. His eyes were expressive, drawing the observer in. Right now they seemed rather despondent, enough to make Penelope want to comfort him. Whatever the maid had told him seemed to have caused quite the wound.

Pen waited until he was well away from the Whitley household, and thus any prying ears or eyes, before she neared him. He was still in what looked like a confounded daze as she "accidentally" bumped into him.

"Oh, forgive me!"

"No, no, it's my fault entirely, I should be paying more attention to where I was going," he said, gallantly removing his hat and lowering his head in apology.

"Let's just chalk it up to happenstance," she said with a forgiving smile. "Are you a friend of the Whitleys? I saw you leaving their house."

"Whitleys?" he repeated as he donned his hat again. "Um, no, I actually came to see a Susan Bennett, at least I thought I was. Not sure what I'm going to do with these, now."

His frustrated gaze fell to the colorful flowers in his hand. They were a vivid contrast to his gloomy countenance, vibrant pinks, reds, and yellows all charmingly wrapped in newspaper.

"Susan Bennett?" Penelope repeated, a look of thoughtfulness on her face. "And she lives with the Whitleys?"

He drew his eyes back up to Penelope.

"Oh no, she's a relative, coming into town from Cleveland." He gave her a self-effacing smile. "We met on the train to New York yesterday."

"Yesterday?" Well, the Whitleys certainly didn't waste any time getting rid of her. "And she was staying with the Whitleys?"

"That's what she told me. Gave me the address and everything...at least I thought I had the right address."

"Did she say why she was visiting?"

He narrowed his eyes, no doubt starting to get suspicious.

Pen thought quickly.

"I just thought with everything going on with the family, it was a rather interesting time for her to visit. But then again, they must have been very close if she came to visit now of all times." Being that the man obviously didn't know the family, he wouldn't question a perfectly made-up mysterious tragic event Pen had just hinted at. "Is that the impression you got on the train yesterday?"

"The maid denied even knowing her!"

It didn't exactly answer her question, but certainly raised a few more. Maids usually knew every person in the house at any given time. Perhaps she was just loyal to her murderous employers? Or maybe they had threatened her?

"And you're sure you have the right address?"

"Absolutely, I made sure to commit it to memory."

"I know sometimes women give out wrong information for their own safety." Or if they have no interest in a man and simply want an easy way to quickly rid themselves of the nuisance, Penelope thought.

"But we seemed to get along so well," he said, looking thoroughly perplexed. "We spent hours talking in the dining car."

"Is that where you first met her?"

A humble smile appeared on his face, endearing Pen to him. She could see how a woman could fall for him.

"She was being hassled by some young degenerate. I offered to intervene on her behalf. He seemed to take that as a challenge and asked if I planned on doing something about it. I have no idea where it came from but I stood my ground. Told him to go ahead and try it on, which was enough to have him back down. I know from a few experiences growing up that most bullies are all bark and no bite. After that, I invited her for a coffee in the dining car, and...

the rest is history." He stared past her toward the Whitley residence. "I suppose that descriptor is rather literal at this point, being that I now have no way to find her."

Penelope wasn't about to be the one to tell him that his Susan Bennett may very well be dead.

"I have an idea. I live in this neighborhood," she lied. "Perhaps I could keep an eye out for her. If I see her, I can ask about you, Mr....?"

"David Cranberry."

"Cranberry?"

"I know, quite fanciful. Why do you think I was bullied so much as a kid?" He laughed.

Pen smiled. She knew how cruel children could be. A boy with the last name Cranberry would certainly do the trick.

"Well, Mr. Cranberry, I hate to see such a fortuitous meeting end in such an abysmal manner. As I said, I'd be more than happy to keep an eye out for this Susan and let her know you're *desperately seeking* her."

He grinned at Penelope's dramatic tone. "Why thank you."

"So then, what does your Miss Bennett look like?"

"She has red hair the color of fire," he said wondrously. "It was wavy when I saw her, cut down to her chin. She's about five-foot-six, with—pardon my frankness—a very nice set of gams. But that isn't the part that attracted me to her. She had the most beautiful eyes you've ever seen, so green you could spot them from across the room. An amazing smile, and the way she crinkles her nose when she laughs is just..."

He was so dizzy for the dame he was practically reeling on his feet. But the way his eyes reflected everything he said so ardently, it was enough to make even Penelope's heart go pitter-pat.

Unfortunately, this did indeed resemble her dead woman, at least the part about her hair. Granted the rain had darkened it some, but it was the right length.

"Was there anything else that might identify her?"

He thought for a moment. "Yes! She wore a gold chain bracelet with a charm on it. It was a music note, which I thought was unusual. She told me her mother had given it to her and she was wearing it for good luck. She kept fiddling with it while I was with her. I think she was nervous about the train ride."

Pen thought of the woman she had seen and didn't recall a bracelet. Depending on how thin it was, it would have been hard to spot a bracelet on her wrist from so far away, especially with all the rain.

"Well, that certainly helps. Is there anything else you can tell me about her?"

"Only that those three hours with her were the most interesting conversation I've ever had with a woman—with anyone really. Please be sure to tell her that."

"Three hours? My, she really must have made an impression on you, and obviously you on her as well."

Penelope was awfully curious about what Susan had said during those three hours, but she was already dancing the line between curious and suspiciously intrusive.

"And how should I get in touch with you Mr. Cranberry? Are you at a hotel in town?"

"Oh no, I live here. I can give you the phone number to my apartment building. It's a communal phone, just ask for me if you call."

"Had Susan planned on moving here?"

He wrinkled his brow in confusion.

"I mean if she's from Cleveland and you live here, then..."

"Ah yes," he said with a chuckle. "You know, in our conversation, it never came up, can you believe that?"

No, Pen couldn't believe that at all. It must have been *some* conversation. Still, it was a small matter.

"I guess I'm a believer in true love. When you find the right woman, not even distance should be a barrier." He looked down at the flowers in one hand. "I suppose I might as well give you these for your kind effort, Miss...?"

"Banks. Penelope Banks."

"Miss Banks, here you go."

After handing her the flowers. " I don't have anything to write my number down on, unfortunately."

"That's no matter, I'm good at remembering. You can just tell me."

"Oh, well, I suppose so." He rattled off the number, then gave her an uncertain look.

"And...memorized," she said cheerily, having visualized all the numbers in her head to better remember them. He still looked skeptical.

"If she doesn't want to see me, I'll understand, and I have no problem with you calling me up and telling me as much. I just want to make sure nothing has happened to her."

Penelope debated telling him the unfortunate news then and there, but once again decided against it. It didn't really seem her place. Surely this infatuation would pass. He'd only met the woman yesterday, after all. A handsome man like this, if a bit too romantic for his own good, would have no problem catching the eye of another woman to soothe his sorrow. Perhaps she'd indulge him in *four* hours of conversation?

"Thank you, Miss Banks. I know it seems silly but...I just have this feeling about her."

"So do I," Penelope said, feeling perfectly awful.

At some point perhaps she'd tell him. For now, she had to find out exactly what had happened to this Susan Bennett.

CHAPTER NINE

"THESE ARE FOR YOU, MY SWEET," PENELOPE SAID, handing Jane the bouquet of flowers David Cranberry had given her.

"Oh, how lovely!"

"Nothing for moi?" Benny asked with an exaggerated pout.

"I know you were spying on us the whole time. Surely that was enough to satisfy your prurient needs?"

"It was hardly that scandalous. So, what did you learn?"

"Her name is Susan Bennett and she came in on a train only yesterday!"

Both Jane and Benny were expectedly surprised by this.

"At least according to this David Cranberry."

"Cranberry? What a lovely last name." Jane sighed, no doubt thinking about her own slightly more unfortunate surname.

"It is rather precious. And from what I spied via these glasses, he was rather toothsome to boot, though he could use a good spiffing up. I should introduce him to my tailor."

"Let's not scare him off too quickly. I may have to reconnect with him at some point, if only to give him the bad news. He was here to meet Susan, who certainly fits the description of the woman I saw last night. He met her on the train."

"How awful!" Jane lamented. "So you didn't tell him she might be dead?"

"It didn't seem like my place. Also, I'm not entirely sure about him."

"Oh, Pen, you suspect everyone when you're in the middle of an investigation."

"For good reason. I've learned my lesson from quite a few of my cases, thank you."

"So you suspect this Cranberry fellow of sneaking into Washington Square Park, perhaps to meet with his lady love...at two in the morning...in the middle of a thunderstorm...only to kill her? To what end?"

"I didn't say he killed her, but..." Pen sighed, unable to put her finger on exactly what it was that bothered her about him. Perhaps it was the speed at which the courtship moved. He met Susan on the train yesterday and today he was bringing flowers?

Granted, her own past had made her biased against whirlwind romances. She and Clifford Stokes had only known each other for a few months before she agreed to marry him, only to find him with Constance the day before their vows were to take place.

"It doesn't matter," Pen said, waving it away. "Did you see anything interesting while I was sleuthing?"

"Only some absurd boy across the way riding, of all things, a penny-farthing."

"Really?" Pen said with a laugh, craning her neck to look at the other side of the park.

Sure enough, there was a man atop one of those ridiculous bicycles with one large wheel and a smaller one behind it.

"I'd be terrified of falling over," Jane said.

"I didn't even see people using those when I was a girl. He's quite agile with it, though."

"Which tells you this isn't his first time. It's probably his literal mode of transportation! I never understood certain young people's fascination with the obsolete and old-fashioned. I'll bet he's the type to eschew anything modern and make a point of telling anyone within hearing distance. Don't get me wrong, I too long for a simpler, more genteel era on occasion. I always thought I'd look quite toffee in a good stovepipe hat or a tweed ulster. Whatever happened to capes for men?"

"I'm not sure how enjoyable that past would have been for any of us sitting here. I, for one, can't wait to see what the future will bring." Pen turned back to the Whitley residence. "But enough of penny-farthings and stovepipe hats. I'm beginning to think we need to be less passive about this. I need to find a way into that house. Right now it seems—"

Penelope was cut short as they all noted the arrival of Detective Prescott at the front steps of the Whitley residence.

"Well, it's about time," Penelope said. It had to be well past eleven by now. Who knew what they could have been up to in that house?

Pen took hold of the opera glasses which afforded a much closer view of the maid after she answered the door. There was an apprehensive look on her face, though Pen couldn't necessarily attribute that to guilt. Anyone would be wary of a detective coming to their front door. Still, for a detective, she nodded and opened the door wider for him to enter.

"Wonderful," she said, setting her glasses down after the door closed behind him. "Perhaps he'll finally get some answers."

Now that something seemed to be happening to move the case along, Penelope grabbed a sandwich to nibble on. She relaxed to enjoy the thickly cut ham and cheddar, realizing that she was famished.

It was short-lived as Detective Prescott exited the home not ten minutes later.

"Zounds! That was hardly long enough to even question someone."

"Is he coming our way?"

"I think he sees us."

Penelope had noticed the same thing, which now took precedence over his far too short interview with the Whitleys. The look on his face indicated that yes, he had noticed them.

"Hello Detective Prescott," Jane greeted, looking at him with the adoring eyes of a puppy.

Benny had an entirely different look in his eyes as he greeted him. "Detective Prescott, fancy seeing you here."

"Miss Pugley," he said, offering Jane a charming smile.

"Mr. Davenport," he added with a wry twist of the lips toward Benny.

For Penelope, he reserved a look of pure resignation. "And Miss Banks, of course."

"Detective, how lovely to see you again," she said pleasantly.

"I suppose I should have taken you at your word that you would be here. I *was* happy to learn that you haven't been harassing the Whitleys."

"That makes one of us. I noted how short your visit with

them was. Whatever could they have said to make you give up so easily?"

"Give up? What exactly is it I'm supposed to be giving up? Or is this you asking whether or not I questioned them about a body that seems to have vanished into thin air?"

"Yes, if you'd like to put it that way," Pen responded testily.

"No, I didn't."

Penelope opened her mouth to protest, but he held up a hand to silence her. He swiveled his head toward the arch.

"How high would you say that is?"

"If you're questioning my distance vision or memory, I can assure you there is nothing wrong with either."

"I just wonder how well both your vision and memory might hold up in, say, a police lineup."

"I'd be willing to put it to the test," she scoffed.

"I thought you might say that."

"Detective, really, if you're going to stand there and question my integrity and abilities, I'm afraid I'll have to ask that *you* stop harassing *us* on this fine day as we enjoy the perfectly harmless activity of picnicking."

"And here I thought you were spying," he said, not bothering to hide an amused smile.

"And if I was, it would be rather difficult to be incognito while chatting with a detective. A bit conspicuous wouldn't you say? Not that you aren't a lovely vision," she added, batting her eyelashes in an affected manner.

"Perhaps you'd rather come with me instead?"

"Am I under arrest?" she asked with a mixture of alarm and outrage. Surely what she was doing wasn't illegal?

"No, but I'm hoping you'll join me so we can perhaps put this matter to rest. Unless of course, you'd rather sit out here all day hoping to find something that confirms your suspicions. I'd say even with two blankets, at some point your enjoyable little picnic is going to be a rather wet affair."

"It is getting rather marshy, Pen," Benny said.

"Where are you taking me?" Penelope asked with suspicion.

"The Whitleys have agreed to meet with you."

"They *have*?"

That had all of them sitting up a little straighter in surprise.

"They have. Like you, they would like some finality to this for once and for all."

Penelope narrowed her eyes at the detective, then slid them past his shoulder to the Whitley home. Were they watching right now, already getting their stories aligned?

Still, how could she refuse this offer?

"Fine," she said, smoothing down her skirt before standing up.

She faltered as her heel once again sank into the grass. Detective Prescott was quick, instinctively reaching his arm out to curl around her waist before she teetered over.

Jane giggled with delight.

Benny chuckled suggestively.

"Careful where you step, Miss Banks," Detective Prescott said, his thickly-lashed eyes staring right at her as his mouth hitched up on one side.

"I'm quite sure of my footing," she said smartly. As much as she enjoyed the feel of his arm around her waist, she hated that it came at the expense of her self-assurance.

What exactly was going on here?

He held onto her long enough to get her on the firmer footing of the path, then she shrugged out of his embrace if only to regain her composure.

"So, did they espy me as well?" she asked as he led her back toward the home.

"They didn't, actually. I was the one to suggest they meet with you, that you might just happen to be in the area."

"Why would they agree to meet with me? William Whitley didn't seem too pleased with me last night."

"Could you blame him, considering the hour?"

"I suppose not. I still don't like this. It feels like an ambush."

Detective Prescott's only response was a soft chuckle of amusement. It only infuriated Penelope, but at this point, she was too proud to ask for an explanation. Considering how cryptic he was being, she doubted she'd get one.

She followed him up the steps to the front door. He knocked twice before it was instantly opened by the same maid she had seen open the door all morning.

"Detective." Her eyes slid to Penelope and hardened somewhat.

"Penelope Banks," she greeted with a polite smile.

"Yes, ma'am. Please come in."

The maid opened the door wider for them, then led them to the parlor which looked out onto the park. The windows had all been curtained this morning and still were. Still, there was plenty of light filtering in through the thin material.

It was enough for Penelope to see exactly why her presence had been requested.

CHAPTER TEN

PENELOPE STARED AT WHAT SHE ASSUMED WAS THE entirety of the Whitley family in the parlor. The resemblance was unmistakable.

Everyone in the room had red hair of various shades, from pale reddish blond to flaming orange to a coppery gold. Even William's hair, which she had deemed more blond than strawberry last night, now looked quite the opposite in the filtered midday sun.

There were five of them in total, two men and three women. Each one stared back with varying looks of satisfaction, which was understandable.

They had won the battle, it would seem.

"Do you happen to recognize anyone in the room?" Detective Prescott asked. To his credit, he didn't sound patronizing or taunting. Penelope was certain he believed what she had told him about the body, or he at least believed that *she* believed it was true.

And she still did.

"No, I don't," she said firmly. She turned to Detective

Prescott with an adamant look. "No one in this room is the woman I saw last night."

"And just what is it you were up to last night?" William asked in an insinuating manner.

Penelope turned back toward him and narrowed her eyes. "A party with friends."

"With plenty of illegal alcohol I'm sure," he scoffed.

The other man in the room, several years younger, mid-twenties perhaps, with similarly thinning hair in a shade of overly ripe carrots snickered.

"*Quiet*, Andrew," William muttered.

Andrew was more handsome, mostly because the super-cilious airs of his brother were replaced by a far more care-free bearing. He lazed back on the couch with an expression of amusement coloring his face. Still, his twinkling blue eyes scanned Penelope up and down in a way she didn't particu-larly like.

William gave Detective Prescott an exasperated look. "Really Detective, surely this is enough to convince you that this woman was either too drunk to know what she saw, or she's making this up for some nefarious reason."

"I'm not convinced of anything," Detective Prescott said, giving him a look that had the man drawing in his claws. He turned back to Penelope with a softer expression. "All the same, Miss Banks, are you certain that, what with the rain, the time of night, and...other factors, you might not have mistaken one of the Whitleys for the woman you saw?"

"I don't know," she said, turning to give the family a sardonic look. "Did any of you ladies happen to find your-self lying next to the fountain outside, either stabbed or shot?"

"Stabbed?" repeated the one sitting to the side in a

chair. She was the prettiest in the room, striking even, with hair the color of gold reflecting the setting sun. Her clear blue eyes stared at Penelope with unease as she instinctively brought her hand up to her chest.

"Pull yourself together, Tallulah," William gritted out. "There was no body by the fountain."

"There was," Penelope insisted.

"And where is it now?"

"Perhaps *you* can tell me? It seems to have disappeared."

"Every female member of this household has been in this house all morning, very much alive," William said.

"My husband had nothing to do with any woman by the fountain, and frankly—"

"It's fine, Caroline," William said, patting the knee of the woman next to him, which made Penelope think perhaps she was his wife rather than a blood relative. She had hair that was a bright auburn color. Zounds, they even married the same! "These accusations are nothing more than the meaningless rambles of a hysterical woman who—"

"*Hysterical?*"

"—has no proof of any misdeed, or that this *supposed* woman even existed in the first place."

"Susan Bennett," Penelope blurted out, studying them all carefully. "I'm sure that name means something to you."

William was able to maintain a steady, insolent gaze upon her, as did his wife. The way the other three members of the family instinctively caught each other's eyes told her they knew the name.

"Susan Bennett?" Detective Prescott inquired.

"Perhaps I should let the Whitleys tell you who she is?" she hinted, arching an eyebrow their way.

Most of them had a firm set to their mouths. The

woman who seemed to be the youngest—pretty in a saucy sort of way, with bobbed hair in a bright copper color, like an overly polished penny— laughed and rolled her eyes.

"She's our cousin."

"Ruth!" William snapped.

"What? Do you want us to lie with a detective here?" She turned back to Penelope and Detective Prescott. "Susan Bennett is our father's sister's only daughter."

"Our father who is *quite ill*, I might add," William insisted. "This business is doing nothing for his health."

Penelope's eyes flashed toward the stairs. Presumably, their father was on bedrest in one of the rooms upstairs. Had he seen or heard anything? Did he even exist?

Her mind really was wandering down the path of perfect insanity. She needed to corral it, if only to bring justice to the woman she was absolutely certain she saw last night.

"Could it have been her Miss Banks saw last night?" Detective Prescott asked.

"No, it could *not* have been," William said in a terse voice. "Our cousin lives in Cleveland."

"Cleveland?" Pen said. That clicked with what David had said.

"Yes, that is where she *lives*," William said.

"But she *will* be here tomorrow," Ruth added in a teasing tone.

Her oldest brother was obviously displeased with this revelation. Still, he used it to his advantage.

"Exactly. In fact, I purchased the ticket for her myself. Which means she couldn't possibly have been here last night, or dead by the fountain for that matter."

Tallulah inhaled sharply at the mention of death again.

William's jaw tightened in response, but he refrained from cautioning her again.

"That's odd since I just spoke with a man, David Cranberry, who claimed he was on the same train as Susan Bennett; a train that came into New York *yesterday*. In fact, he came to your front door only about twenty minutes ago, no doubt claiming as such. Yet your maid claimed she didn't even know the woman."

"Indeed she did. It's no secret that our family has money, and anyone willing to do a bit of research will learn that we have a cousin in Cleveland. It was quite obvious that he was only interested in one thing, and he left quite disappointed."

"He wouldn't be the first fortune-hunting charlatan to show up on our doorstep, right Tully?" Andrew said, shooting his beautiful sister a wink.

Tallulah snapped her attention to him with a wounded look on her face.

"You should talk, Arty, how many times have you gone to pa*pah* with your hat in hand?" Ruth taunted with a grin.

"Will all of you *shut up!*" William hissed.

"So, Susan Bennett wasn't here last night?" Penelope pressed.

"No," he said, giving her an even look.

"I know what I saw and the woman in the window, getting slapped I might add, wasn't anyone in this room."

Penelope noted the way Tallulah's hand rose to her face and her eyes fluttered in surprise when she mentioned the slap. Ruth instinctively turned to look in her oldest brother's direction, with an incredulous accusatory look. Andrew just sighed and rolled his eyes. William and his wife Caroline both remained impassive.

"I think it's time that you left, Miss Banks. We've

indulged your wild accusations and fanciful imaginings long enough." William slid his eyes to Detective Prescott. "I assume this settles the matter? When our cousin arrives *tomorrow* you, and you *alone*, are welcome to come and verify her status as very much alive."

Before Penelope could so much as open her mouth to pose another question, Detective Prescott spoke.

"Thank you for indulging us, Mr. Whitley. Miss Banks and I both understand you were under no obligation to allow us into your home, and we are both grateful. We'll leave you to your day."

Penelope turned to him with incredulity.

"Miss Banks," he said tightly, already placing a hand on her arm to guide her back toward the front door.

She reluctantly allowed it, realizing that there wasn't much more to be discovered, at least from questioning the family. Still, her eyes wandered, wondering if somewhere in this house the body had been hidden away.

"No resemblance to anyone in that house, my foot!" She protested as soon as they were outside with the door closed on them. "Every woman in there resembles her— but *isn't* her! He set that up just to make me look like some silly, overly imaginative twit."

"You certainly had quite the busy morning. You couldn't have shared this information about Susan Bennett and Dave Cranberry with me?"

"Only because you saw fit to lead me directly into an ambush!" Pen said, still fuming.

"An ambush?" He replied, his mouth subtly curling in that infuriating way that told her he was holding back a grin.

"It was an attack of the redheads! You knew all of them being ginger-haired would cast doubt on my claims. Well, it didn't work. I know the woman I saw last night and she was not in that house!"

"You are right in one regard, it does cast doubt on your claim. You have no body, the woman you suspect it might have been seems to be alive and still on her way here to New York according to them. Then there's the matter of your state of inebriation last night."

Penelope gasped with outrage.

Detective Prescott held up a hand before she could unleash it on him. "I'm looking at this from a strictly procedural point of view. What jury on earth would convict any of them based on the evidence you have?"

"So get a warrant to search their home."

"With what probable cause? Even the most lax judge wouldn't sign a warrant for that based solely on your claims."

"What about Dave Cranberry? He can attest to the fact that a Susan Bennett was on the train here yesterday, and matches the description I gave."

"The one who showed up unannounced claiming he met a mysterious woman who claimed to be their cousin?"

"Well...yes," Penelope said, feeling her frustration set in. She couldn't deny what he was arguing. All William would have to do is spin his tale about a fortune hunter.

"As it is, I'm afraid there really isn't a case to investigate. At least until someone comes forward to report this woman missing."

"So it would seem," she snapped in a petty tone.

"All the same, knowing what I do about you, I'm sure you'll continue investigating. If what you say happened really did happen, it means there is a murderer on our hands, or at least someone who is desperate to cover up an accident that may be their fault. I strongly suggest you keep that in mind. Desperation erodes quite a few inhibitions."

"Thank you for the warning, *detective*."

He stared at her, the usual look of exasperation on his handsome face. Penelope returned her usual unconvincing smile of appeasement.

Her eyes darted back toward the house, wondering how she could find a way in.

"Allow me to escort you back to your picnic. I wouldn't want you to suffer another misstep, Miss Banks," Detective Prescott said, giving her a pointed look.

Her eyes flitted back to him and narrowed. "I know exactly where my feet are at all times, and I can use them to walk myself back, thank you very much. Good day!"

She spun around and waited for traffic to clear before crossing the street to head back to the park. She could feel his eyes on her the whole way back to her blanket.

She could also feel the eyes of the Whitleys on her. She was more certain than ever that the death wasn't an accident, or at least had some sinister plot attached to it. Everyone in that parlor had been hiding something.

And Penelope planned on finding out what it was.

CHAPTER ELEVEN

BOTH BENNY AND JANE WERE STARING WITH EAGER eyes as Penelope approached the blanket. She made sure to step carefully over the damnably pliant sod before falling down next to them.

"I saw you and Detective Prescott arguing. What was that about?" Jane asked. She had opened the bottled ginger beer and poured some into a metal cup.

"The entire house is filled with dastardly gingers," Pen said, in a rather huffy way. Truthfully, she was quite fond of red hair, at least in certain hues. Tallulah in particular sported a shade that should have made most women green with envy, at least if red hair were a more popular characteristic.

"They're *all* redheads?" Benny asked.

"It does make sense if they're related. So was one of them the woman you saw?" Jane asked.

"Not at all. And they are all definitely hiding something. It seems Susan Bennett is set to arrive *tomorrow*."

"So who came yesterday?"

"That's what I intend to find out," Penelope said, grabbing a cup and pouring herself some ginger beer.

"An impersonator, how thrilling!" Benny said, looking perfectly intrigued. "You never cease to entertain, Pen."

She pursed her lips with irritation. She wasn't finding this quite as enjoyable as her friend.

"Either an impersonator or she was the real Susan Bennett and they lied. They're denying she was ever at the house at all!"

"I would imagine most families would rather not have the taint of death tied to their name. They probably think the whole affair is already scandalous enough as it is, at least on that side of the park. The rest of the neighborhood knows no shame, and God bless them for it," Benny lifted his own cup toward the south part of the park where 5th Avenue became Thompson Street.

"Speaking of scandalous, it looks like the rebel of the family is making an escape," Penelope said.

Ruth Whitley had a satchel over her shoulder, the kind used to hold books and papers, as she left the house and skipped across the street to the park. She was headed in the direction of the fountain, but before she crossed 5th Avenue, she made a point of deliberately turning to face the trio having a picnic. She grinned, winked, and tauntingly saluted Penelope. With a laugh, she then dodged the car traffic in the middle of the park to head toward the fountain.

"Definitely the black sheep," Penelope muttered.

But was she a murderer?

Penelope watched as Ruth headed straight for the same group of law students she had been talking to earlier. She frowned in confusion. Ruth seemed a bit young to be in law school. Penelope had pegged her as not even twenty yet, but perhaps she had been wrong.

At any rate, Ruth seemed to be awfully chummy with the boys, boldly taking the cigarette from Cal and sticking it into her own mouth to take a puff.

They all chatted for a while, or rather flagrantly flirted with one another. Georgie seemed particularly taken with her, and Ruth didn't seem to be dismissive about it. Only Alfie seemed immune to her kittenish display.

Cal stood to pluck his cigarette back out of her mouth. She pouted, just before tilting her head and saying something to him. He shrugged and pulled a pack out of his pocket. She plucked her own cigarette. Rather than wait for him to light it, she boldly shoved her hand into one pocket, then the other until she found a gold lighter to do it herself.

Ruth fell onto Thomas's lap as she lit her cigarette. He said something to her and she threw her head back in exasperation. The rest of them began debating all over again, probably about that monkey trial. Ruth obviously wasn't interested. She popped up from Thomas's lap. Before she could leave, Georgie pulled her back by the arm. He leaned in to whisper something in her ear and she grinned, nodded, then skipped away dragging heavily on her cigarette.

Penelope watched as she headed in the direction of the Washington Square College located at the southeast corner of the park.

"Well, that explains it."

"Explains what?" Jane asked.

"Ruth seems to be a student at the NYU undergraduate building, Washington Square College. It's rather experimental."

"How so?"

"Well, the main undergraduate campus for New York

University is up in the Bronx. A shame really, so many students miss out on the rich cultural experience of living down here. It seems the powers that be agreed and commandeered that lone building you see over there on the southeast corner as a standalone campus. They've hired all sorts of interesting figures to teach, which makes me wonder why it isn't vastly more popular. Don't get me wrong, it *was* very convenient to have the main undergrad campus so far north when I attended Barnard up in Morningside Heights." She offered a conspiratorial smile before leaning in closer. "Let's just say, the twain did in fact meet, and quite often. Mostly when I got bored of Columbia boys."

Jane and Benny snickered.

"New York University was my first choice of schools, of course. Naturally, my father wasn't about to send me to a coeducational school. Even my mother couldn't battle him on that front."

Thinking about her mother and her days in college caused Penelope to take a moment to ruminate about the past. Her mother had been one of the victims of the Spanish Flu when Penelope was a sophomore. In the years that followed her death, Penelope had become even more rebellious than before, dropping out of college and living the life of a reckless sybarite who made the flappers of today look like saints.

It had all culminated in her whirlwind and ill-fated romance with Clifford Stokes. That was apparently the final straw on a rather large bale of hay that caused her father to cut her off. He thought a few months of poverty would have her straightening up her act and running back to him.

Instead, she'd become perhaps more sinful than ever, gambling at cards in clubs and speakeasies to make a living.

Though she had to admit, she certainly had grown up during those three years.

Pen focused once again on the law students, who seemed to be done with their time at the fountain and were now headed east in her direction.

"I'll be right back," she said, standing up once again.

As Penelope neared them, she debated which of the young men to approach. Once again she felt Alfred was the best option. She certainly didn't want to lead the others on.

"Alfie!" Pen called out, waving to get his attention.

The others stopped along with him, staring her way and then turning to give him bewildered glances. Alfred just stared at her in guileless surprise as he approached her.

"Penelope Banks, I realized I never gave you my name." She smiled broadly as she held her hand out to shake. He took it, but the quizzical look remained on his face.

"Alfred Paisley."

"My, what a gorgeous last name. So, are you going to this gathering tonight that Georgie mentioned?"

"Well, ah," he considered her with a wary look, as though worried about why she was asking. "I had planned to, at least for a few hours."

"Berries! So, where is it being held? In one of those old factory buildings?" she asked, waving her hand toward the east side of the park which was gradually transitioning into nicer apartments and office spaces, mostly gobbled up as professional campuses for New York University.

His brow creased with dismay. "I'm not sure it's the kind of gathering you'd be interested in, Miss Banks."

Now she was very interested. Anything that had the whiff of controversy automatically intrigued her.

"Please, call me Penelope. What gathering would this be?"

"Georgie calls it his mid-week congress. Those of us studying for the bar take over the place on Wednesday nights. It's mostly a lot of drinking and the Socratic method. I don't think you'd find it very interesting."

"Why Alfie, is that you trying to dissuade me from going? Worried about my precious virtue?"

His wonderful eyes fluttered behind his glasses in confusion. "Well, no, it's just that you seemed rather annoyed by our debating earlier. Still, the location isn't exactly the kind of place for, ah..."

"Proper ladies?"

"Well, yes."

"Fortunately, I'm nothing of the sort. Is Ruth going?" she asked with widely innocent eyes.

"Of course, she always does. But—" He sighed with a cynical air. "That's Ruth."

"There then! I'd love to surprise her, she and I are old acquaintances." Did an hour count?

"It's at the Golden Swan," he said, gauging her reaction.

"Really?" Pen said, breathing out a laugh. Now she understood why he was so hesitant to tell her. "You don't strike me as the Black and Tan sort, Alfie!"

Instead of blushing as she expected, he became visibly upset, angry even.

"Yes, I know the reputation it has. A lot of people like to dwell on the whole *Black and Tan* aspect and other seedy bits, mostly muckrakers and bluenoses. There is that element, but there are also some very interesting conversations that take place. These clubs are one of the few places in this city where you can find a cornucopia of ideas, viewpoints, opinions, you name it, and some semblance of equality! It's intellectually stimul—er, *enlightening*. I plan on practicing criminal law, and not just the usual elitist, upper-crust muckoety-muck. For my purposes, that kind of edification is invaluable."

His passion and eloquence about the matter made him all the more attractive.

"Why that's swell, Alfie. I dabble a bit in criminal justice myself. All the more reason for me to go, wouldn't you say? About what time does Ruth usually make an appearance?"

"You're involved in criminal justice?"

"Private investigator. I'm actually on a case right now."

"So all that talk about a body was a real case?"

"I'm afraid so."

"Do you think Ruth...?"

"Is the murderer? No, of course not," Penelope lied. "What time do you think she'll be there again?"

"She usually swims in around eleven or so, stays until morning, or whenever Calvin or Georgie leaves. Sometimes Thomas if she wants to make them jealous, which is often enough." He sported a look of disapproval.

Boy, she really put the Ruth in ruthless, Pen thought.

"The password to get in tonight will be *res ipsa*, it's a legal term."

"The thing speaks for itself," Pen translated, having had a decent amount of Latin education like any privileged child. "Perfect, thanks so much, Alfie. I suppose I'll see you there."

He still looked uncertain. "If you insist."

"Don't tell Ruth, okay? I'd like to surprise her."

"Of course. I should get back to studying."

"Ta-ta!" she sang, wriggling her fingers in a wave before spinning around to rejoin Benny and Jane.

"And just what was that bit of Mata Hari?" Benny asked one eyebrow raised in amusement when she returned.

"How do you feel about going to the Golden Swan with me tonight?"

Benny understandably sat all the way up in surprise at that invitation. "Is that where those law boys are up to? And to think, they looked so perfectly straitlaced from here. But then, they *are* always the ones aren't they?"

"What's the Golden Swan?" Jane asked.

"A bacchanal hovel of the most debauched kind," Benny crooned.

Jane looked both perplexed and concerned.

"Don't listen to Benny, he loves throwing firecrackers into the fishpond," Penelope said. "Still, he does have a point about this place. While your repertoire of New York experiences could be a bit more *robust*, I think perhaps taking you to the Golden Swan might be tossing you right into the Atlantic just to teach you how to swim."

"I can stomach it," Jane scoffed, not very convincingly. "I'm not *that* much of a wilting violet."

"Not to worry dove, I'll be there to protect your precious petals," Benny said, patting her knee.

"Is it a...*brothel?*" Jane asked, suddenly looking as though she regretted being so bold.

Both Penelope and Benny laughed.

"Perhaps once upon a time, or close enough," Pen confessed.

"A brothel, a boxing ring, a French *salon*, a gambling house, an *ahem* atmosphere where *certain* gentlemen can gather, or just a place to lubricate the parched throat."

"These days it's mostly the latter though. A speakeasy that is very liberated in terms of who they allow access."

"Which is all the more reason for Jane to come. She *should* be exposed to a Black and Tan club, before they completely disappear."

"Why is it called a Black and Tan club?"

Benny answered for her.

"That part of New York, south of Washington Square, is mostly colored and immigrant. Neither group is allowed to be too picky about with whom or where they associate. Thus, you'll often find them converging in the same spots, Irish, Italian, Chinese, Colored, et cetera, et cetera all races drinking together in harmony. Hence the label Black and Tan, a moniker mucked up by some bottom-feeding journalist decades ago to frighten the prigs, a term which they now embrace."

"Where is it?"

"Not too far from here actually," Pen answered. "Right on 6th and 4th Street."

"It really does make one wonder, doesn't it?" Benny mused as he looked around. "A mere patch of grass and a few iconic structures are all that separate the high hat crowd of The Row from the *hoi polloi*."

"That's the beauty of Washington Square."

"Oh, I'd love to go with you tonight," Jane pleaded.

"Then go you shall," Penelope said, ignoring Benny as he smirked and subtly shook his head behind Jane. "That was easy enough. Now for the hard part."

"What's that?"

"Persuading Lulu to go as well."

CHAPTER TWELVE

BENNY, JANE, AND PENELOPE WERE IN THE PEACOCK club later that night where Lucille "Lulu" Simmons was performing as she usually did from Thursday to Saturday night. She was a jazz singer who had helped Penelope during the years she had played cards to make a livable income after her father cut her off.

Penelope had instructed each of her cohorts, including her chauffeur, Leonard, who would also be experiencing a long night, to spend the afternoon getting their sleep in. She had no idea how long this "mid-week congress" at the Golden Swan would be, but knowing what she did about places like that and the fortitude of the average longwinded intellectual who was enamored of his own brilliance, it could go well into the morning.

But first, she had to overcome this obstacle.

When Lulu was done with her set, her gaze immediately homed in on their table, and she came over to join them. Though in Lulu's case, it was more like slinking over, the way a cat would. She looked gorgeous as always in a green silk dress. There was an intricately beaded design that ran down the middle. It matched the beading of the loose waistline that separated the emerald green top from the gauzy lighter green of the bottom. She had a matching beaded head wrap with a black feather.

A bit fancy for the Golden Swan, but whatever made Lulu stand out—and this was a woman who always stood out—could only be a good thing for tonight's purposes.

Penelope had wanted the rest of them to fit in, blending into the background. She had on a more understated-than-usual dress in midnight blue velvet with minimal adornment and a matching cloche hat with nothing more than a grosgrain band around it. Jane, on the other hand, had needed to borrow a dress from Penelope so as not to stand out like a daisy among orchids. She wore a dark rose, calf-length, straight-line dress with lace siding, pretty but not overly eye-catching. Ben looked his usual debonair self.

"Hmm, Jane, Benny, and Penelope? Something tells me y'all didn't come just to hear me sing." Her feline eyes narrowed as she took the last empty seat. "Something *also* tells me I'm being set up."

"Remember how you mentioned you wanted to be involved in one of my cases? I have the perfect opportunity for you. It's a murder case." Penelope poured her some of the expensive champagne she had bought purely for the purposes of bribery.

The suspicious look didn't disappear as she took the glass. "Is that so?"

"It'll be fun."

Benny deliberately cleared his throat. Lulu glanced at him then back to Penelope.

"Why don't you get straight to it?"

"After your set tonight, we want you to come to the Golden Swan with us."

"The *Golden Swan?*" She coughed out a laugh. "Now, I *know* it wasn't one of your little debutantes who got herself killed."

"That's the thing, I have no idea who it is that got murdered."

Penelope told her about the events of the previous night, all the way through this morning's adventures.

A wry smile graced Lulu's face. "I knew from the moment I first saw you outsmart that card hustler, you would never be boring, Pen." She laughed softly before sipping her champagne and swallowing. "Fine, what all is it you want me to do?"

"Get a girl talking."

She smiled sardonically. "Not my usual forte."

"Oh stop, there isn't a person, woman or man, on earth who isn't perfectly mesmerized by you. Besides, knowing what little I do about her, this one will come running to you like an adoring puppy, tail furiously wagging."

Lulu sighed. "That sounds tiresome."

"It won't be that bad."

"I'm going!" Jane announced, as though that resolved the issue. She was already one glass of champagne in, which had made her bold.

Lulu gave Penelope a censuring look. "Please tell me you didn't talk this poor thing into going to the Golden Swan."

"She's a big girl, she can handle herself."

"I can," Jane insisted.

"Just wait until you see the clientele, honey."

"Yes, yes, Lulu," Pen said. "However, I've also seen you handle overly pesky men with perfect ease. I'm sure tonight will be no different."

That was enough to make Lulu laugh. They both knew

she didn't suffer fools, and any man who decided to get too forward with her was a fool indeed.

"Besides, I heard a rumor that you own an adorable little ivory-handled gun," Benny purred.

"Your sources are correct, honey." She turned back to Pen. "And if I have to use it, I fully expect you to keep me out of jail."

"The only other people you'll have to handle are law students."

Lulu groaned. "I think I'd prefer the rougher set."

"Welcome to the world of private investigation. One often has to deal with the worst society has to offer, and insufferable academics are definitely the worst. But you only have to get Ruth Whitley talking, find out more about what's going on in that house, who this cousin Susan Bennett of hers is, and hopefully some reason why Ruth or one of her siblings might want her murdered."

"You certainly don't ask much."

"She seemed the most willing to talk. Maybe a bit of giggle juice will get her singing?"

Lulu lifted her glass. "I shall do my best, only for you Pen."

"That's why I love you, Lulu."

Lulu smiled and rolled her eyes.

"Well, ladies, it seems we have quite the adventurous night ahead of us," Benny said, lifting his glass. "Drink up!"

CHAPTER THIRTEEN

AT A LITTLE PAST MIDNIGHT, AFTER LULU WAS DONE performing for the evening, the quartet was crowded in a Rolls Royce Silver Ghost. Leonard was driving them all the way from Harlem down to Washington Square. Lulu, Jane, and Penelope rode in the back and Benny sat in the front passenger side. It was a long enough drive, especially with traffic, even at this time of night, that some of the champagne had worn off for the more experienced drinkers.

"Do you think she'll last the night?" Benny asked, twisted around in his seat to stare at Jane, secured between Lulu and Penelope.

"I'm just daisy!" Jane announced, then giggled.

"We'll get her some water when we get there," Penelope said, her brow wrinkled with concern. Jane had only had two glasses of champagne and already she looked game enough to swing from the chandeliers.

"Have you forgotten where we're going, Pen?" Lulu reminded her. "I'm pretty sure asking for water at the Golden Swan is a criminal offense."

"Then she'll be our resident teetotaler. Surely some people go only for the lark of it without getting zozzled?"

"I can drive her home instead if you like, Miss Banks," Leonard offered.

"No! I'm fine," Jane insisted, looking suddenly sober. "I apologize for my behavior until now, Miss Banks. I'll be a good girl once inside."

"That's just what I'm worried about, honey," Lulu said, patting her knee.

"It's coming up. You said you wanted me to drop you a block away?" Leonard announced. She'd instructed him to stop east of 6th Avenue so they wouldn't be too obvious.

Pen peered out the windows just to make sure that neither the law students nor Ruth were anywhere nearby.

"Yes, this is good."

After they poured out of the car, Penelope turned to address Leonard. "As I said, I'm afraid it will be a long night for you. I'll give you the day off tomorrow to make up for it."

He grinned. "It's not a problem, Miss Banks. I think I'll park closer to the park, might be a more interesting perch from which to bird watch."

Penelope twisted her lips at his shamelessness. By now, she knew how much of a tomcat he was. "Enjoy."

Pen turned to the other three when he left. "Okay, Benny, Jane, and I will go in first since Ruth has already seen us together. Lulu, you follow a few minutes after so she thinks came in on your own. I'll spend the time in between trying to find her so I can give you a description of what she's wearing. Then when you go to the bar, I'll nonchalantly go over and secretly tell you. From there, the job is all yours."

"Right," Lulu said, with a wry smile. "Off you go then!"

"Remember the password to get in is *res ipsa*," Penelope

said as she slipped Lulu more than enough kale to buy herself drinks.

Penelope hooked her arm through Jane's. Benny took her other arm and they walked down 4th Street toward 6th Avenue.

The Golden Swan had been particularly popular prior to Prohibition. The old saloon still stood, looking like a ghost of itself, at least from the outside. Penelope had never been here back then. As precocious as she was in her youth, even she had been warned off by the tales of murder, thievery, and other crimes this area had been rife with. Theodore Roosevelt, as police commissioner had taken particular interest in the area, flooding it with police to stamp out the worst of it. That only added a patina of danger that still made it a popular destination for thirst hounds and thrill seekers.

Penelope knocked on the door and waited. When a tiny window slid open, she gave the password.

"Res ipsa."

The window immediately closed shut and a second later she heard the bolt unlock. The door opened to a dimly lit space, but Pen could see what remained of the old saloon interior.

The dull sound of chatter and music wafted toward them from somewhere upstairs. She knew that the former owner, Thomas Wallace, had died only three years ago and used to live above the old saloon. The new owners must have taken advantage of that space to turn it into a more secretive location for their illegal speakeasy.

Upstairs, they opened the door and Penelope took a look around. It was all that she had expected and more. The owners had opened up the former apartment by knocking down walls. That created a large space that could accommodate more than the average gin joint. Most speakeasies had sprung up in backrooms, basements, and attics. That was probably why this place could also be louder than other places, where the patrons had to keep their voices down to avoid detection.

In one corner a seemingly thrown-together jazz quartet performed, including one man on the trumpet who Pen assumed was Chinese considering the location. That attested to how mixed the crowd was, and not just in terms of race, though there certainly was that. It was enough to make Penelope understand why Black and Tan saloons had caused such an uproar long before Prohibition set in. There were men dressed in laborer's clothes and right next to them, three men for some reason wearing tuxedos. Artists drew on napkins, gamblers played cards, poets recited their work, locals drowned their sorrows, and quite a few young academic types debated with one another at various tables.

Penelope easily spied her targets in one corner, mostly because Georgie had suddenly jumped up onto the table. He pointed down at Alfie.

"You there, what are the elements that allow for constitutional standing?"

Pen couldn't hear Alfie's response over the music and talking, but the occupants of the tables surrounding them all clapped and roared their approval.

"Hear, hear, drink up!" Georgie shouted before throwing back the drink in his hand.

"I think I've found our group," Pen said, even though she didn't see Ruth's tell-tale red hair among them. "Benny, you watch Jane. I'm going to try and find Ruth somewhere. According to Alfie, she should already be here."

"We'll be at the bar," he said with a devilish grin.

The space was large and quite crowded, but Pen figured

Ruth would be easy enough to spot mostly because of the red hair. She was just thinking about risking it and going to the table to ask about Ruth's whereabouts when she heard a voice behind her.

"You're certainly persistent aren't you?"

Penelope spun around, a pang of guilty surprise pricking her. She was met with a grinning Ruth Whitley, tonight dressed in a dark green dress that showed off her pale arms and perhaps a bit too much décolletage.

"I suppose this means I'm suspect number one?"

CHAPTER FOURTEEN

"Ruth, isn't it?" Penelope said. "What are you doing here?"

"I should ask you the same thing," Ruth replied with a sardonic smile. She looked more amused than upset or irritated.

Before she could respond, Ruth took hold of her hand and dragged her toward the table. "Look boys, we have a gal here who's oh so interested in the law, specifically criminal law. Maybe you all could give her some help?"

Ruth let go of Pen's hand and fell into Cal's lap, throwing her arms around his neck.

"Our fountain nymph! You decided to come after all," Georgie said, now down from the table.

"She's no nymph," Ruth scoffed, smirking at Pen. "She's on the hunt, thinks I'm a murderer."

"Is it the murder you were trying to analyze this morning?" Thomas asked.

"She discussed it with you all?" Ruth asked, giving them a stunned look, then turning back to Pen with narrowed eyes. "Why don't you just take out an ad in the *New York Times*?"

"I can see it now," Georgie said, his hands in the air as though broadcasting a marquee. "Wanted: one missing dead woman. Will entertain all inquiries."

"I hardly think murder is a matter of jocularity," Pen retorted.

"Except, you don't have a body do you?" Ruth asked, one eyebrow arched.

"Not yet," Pen said, giving her a level look.

Ruth just grinned. "Perhaps it really is my cousin! My cousin who was somehow still alive this morning to send a telegram informing us she was arriving tomorrow morning."

"That does pose quite the conundrum," Cal said.

"Maybe tomorrow is yesterday and yesterday is tomorrow," Georgie said with a little jig in his step as he crossed his arms in different directions.

"It could be like something out of that *Time Machine* book by whatshisname," Ruth offered, playing along.

"H.G. Wells," Alfred said in a bored tone.

"Yes!" Georgie said. "She came tomorrow morning, then went back in time to arrive yesterday, only to meet her tragic end."

"In which case, be sure to warn her about her upcoming death tomorrow, Ruthie," Cal said to Ruth in a droll voice.

"Unless I'm the killer," Ruth said, waggling her eyebrows like a villain.

"What would be your motive?" Pen asked with a daring look.

"Ohhh," Georgie said with a laugh. "Be careful of this one, boys. She'd certainly give you a run for your money in any courtroom."

"Exactly why I plan on going into business law," Cal said. "Wealthy clients only, the kind who abhor the publicity of a court case. I plan on making a mint. No sense in mucking about with the bottom-feeders of society who commit more violent crimes."

"You obviously don't know the wealthy as well as you think you do," Penelope remarked with a cynical laugh.

Thomas and Georgie both coughed out laughs as well. Alfie managed a subtle smile. Ruth smirked. Cal scowled.

"That calls for another round. *Garçon!*" Georgie shouted, snapping his fingers.

"There's no waiter, you dunce," Thomas said.

"I'll get the next round," Alfie said, standing up. He deliberately eyed Penelope as though encouraging her to follow.

Once they were out of range, he asked, "Are you truly old friends with Ruth?"

Penelope considered him. She suspected he was a more serious character who could probably be trusted. She also got the impression he wasn't quite as beguiled by Ruth as the other boys were. Even now, Pen could see that Ruth had hopped from Cal's lap to Thomas's, whispering in his ear with a devilish grin in a way that made him shift uncomfortably in his seat.

"No, but she's right, I do consider her a suspect in a murder."

He stared at her unblinking. "I see."

"Miss Banks!" Pen heard Jane exclaim behind her. "They have sherry! Benny bought me a third round. I haven't had this since before Prohi-Prohi*petition?*"

Alfred turned to stare at Jane, his eyes wide with concern and disapproval. Tragically, Jane looked as though Benny had plied her with the entire bottle of sherry. Her long hair, usually neatly done back in her standard soft chignon fell into her face, which was flushed. Her soft blue eyes were glazed and unfocused. Even the rose dress she had on somehow looked disheveled.

Pen flashed an infuriated look Benny's way. He just shrugged as though the whole thing had been completely out of his control.

"What can I do, she drinks them down like water, Pen."

"They're *so* good," Jane cooed, cupping the freshly poured one in her hand.

Alfie frowned and turned his attention back to Pen. "At any rate, if you're trying to get us to help you entrap Ruth, I won't be a party to it. While I'm not exactly as enamored of her as my former classmates seem to be, I still believe in fighting fair, and she's at least a few drinks in already."

"I don't want to take advantage of her, Alfie, but there is still the matter of a murdered woman."

That gave him pause. He stared at her as though debating how to digest that.

Behind him, Pen saw Lulu arrive, gliding her way through the crowd, which automatically parted for her. The dim lighting of the speakeasy made her skin shimmer like burnished copper. She caught Pen's eye and came over to stand behind Alfred at the bar, as though waiting to order a drink.

"At any rate, it seems your element of surprise has been ruined," Alfie finally said. "She's figured you out. Frankly, you weren't exactly subtle about it."

Penelope spoke louder as she responded. "Well, you can tell Ruth that I won't be bothering her anymore tonight. You can also tell her, I think her *dark green* dress does wonders for her red hair."

Lulu gave a subtle nod and smile, telling Pen she knew what dress to look for.

Alfie gave her a confused look, then dismissed it as he ordered another round of drinks for his table and left. Penelope saw Lulu follow him with her gaze.

"Good luck," Pen muttered in passing as she stalked over to handle the perfectly unreliable Benny. He sat next to Jane at a table shared with two quietly morose men who were only focused on their drinks.

Jane was slumped back in her chair, her fresh glass of sherry only half finished. Presumably, she'd succumbed to her low tolerance for alcohol. It was probably for the best.

"Remind me never to put you in charge, should I ever have children."

Benny chuckled. "Has being around Detective Prescott made you broody, Pen?"

She frowned with irritation. The last thing she needed was the distraction of his name. But now she wondered what his views on children were. Not that it mattered. He had yet to even officially invite her to dinner, though he had once hinted he might do so in the near future. After this mess of a case, she doubted such a thing would be forthcoming anytime soon.

Now, Penelope was even more irritated.

Benny laughed, reading it on her face. Pen scowled and turned to the bar and watched as Lulu turned one man after the other down for her attentions. It would be a while before any of the law students or Ruth was back at the bar for her to engage with.

But Lulu was nothing if not creative.

She set her finished drink down and slinked over to the jazz band situated close to the table of law students. One look was all it took to have them coming to a stop.

Pen was amused to see her pick the Chinese trumpet player's ear to whisper into. She had a feeling it was deliberate. He grinned and nodded. One second later the small band started back up.

Penelope recognized the long musical intro to "Everybody Loves My Baby," done in a far jazzier sound than usual. Lulu took her place in front of them, which had anyone who wasn't too far into their cups suddenly paying attention.

Particularly the law students sitting at the nearby table.

Lulu's sultry voice was loud enough to carry even over the band and melodic enough to have everyone on their feet dancing. Ruth lured Georgie onto his feet to dance the Charleston. Even Jane came to enough to beg Benny to take her to the dance floor.

Penelope was more than happy to sit back and watch, finally taking a moment to relax and sip the remainder of Jane's sherry.

When Lulu was done with the song, rewarded with an uproarious round of applause, it was no surprise when she was invited to join the table of law students. Penelope had observed how she'd made subtle, nonverbal eye contact with the members of that table—at least when she wasn't flirting with the trumpet player—and they had easily taken the bait.

"Oh, that was fun!" Jane said, eyes aglow as she and Benny came back.

"She's all yours, Pen," a weary Benny said. His eyes slid to the table of men dressed in tuxedos. "It's my turn to have a bit of enjoyment and leisure." The three men gave him wary looks when he approached the table, then relaxed at something he said and invited him to join them.

Yes, the Golden Swan truly was open to all.

"Thank you so much for this Pen, it's been swell," Jane

said before her head plopped right down onto the table and she was out once again. That at least made her less of a burden to keep an eye on, even though the two men they shared the table with eyed her with disfavor.

Half an hour passed. Ruth was as smitten with Lulu as Pen suspected she would be, all her attention on the jazz singer. Benny was just as happily occupied with his fellow confirmed bachelors. Unfortunately, with no one to occupy her, Pen was threatening to join Jane in blissful, boozy sleep.

She was saved from that fate by a smartly dressed couple who had just entered. Their presence perked Penelope up mostly because she recognized them.

Ducky and Mona didn't see her as they passed through the club and went straight to the table where Ruth and the law students sat.

"Well, well, well, how about that!"

CHAPTER FIFTEEN

"It seems our Ducky has become reacquainted with the neighbors after all," Pen said to herself as she watched Ducky and Mona steal chairs to join Ruth, Lulu, and the table of law students.

Ducky was greeted like an old friend by Ruth in particular, who jumped up from Thomas's lap and hugged him, then planted a kiss on each of Mona's cheeks.

Penelope debated whether or not it was worth making her presence known, but the decision became moot when Ducky rose to get another round of drinks for the table. His eye happened to land on her from across the room.

At first, there was a look of shock, which was quickly stifled by a broad and welcoming smile.

What had that been about? Maybe nothing. Perhaps Pen was reading too much into it.

"Pen, dear! What are you doing at the Golden Swan? And all by yourself? Not wise in an establishment like this," he said as he approached.

"I'm here with Benny," she said, tilting her head in his direction.

"Ah, it seems he's found a group of like-minded fellows. Bully for him. Not so much for you, Pen. Why don't you come and join my table of chums?"

Mona's Britishisms really were influencing him.

Pen thought about saying no. She didn't want Ruth to suddenly stop talking to Lulu due to her sudden appearance.

"I'm actually responsible for this one tonight, as well," she said, pointing to Jane, whose head was still plopped on the table. "But I see you've reacquainted yourself with your neighbors after all?"

His smile faltered, as he no doubt wondered how she knew Ruth. "Well, yes. But Ruthie's hardly a killer, is she? She may have been a complete pest growing up, but that certainly doesn't translate into murder."

"If you say so," Pen said pleasantly. She was too exhausted by now to convince him there might be a murderer among his neighbors. But she could still use him for information. "So you know the Whitleys well? Have they lived on The Row long?"

"They have, for as long as I've been alive. And as far as I know, they are all present and accounted for."

"Including distant relatives? Ruth mentioned a cousin from Cleveland, a Susan Bennett?"

"Hell, Pen, you really do know how to kill a fun evening. I didn't come out tonight to discuss the neighbors' family tree. Come over and you can ask Ruthie yourself. It looks like your friend is finally coming to."

Pen turned to see Jane slowly lifting her head and looking around as though wondering where she was.

"Oh, my head feels like—"

"Carpenters going to work?" Ducky said with a laugh. He lifted his glass toward her. "There's a cure for that!"

Jane blinked in surprise at the perfect stranger before her.

"This is Ducky from last night, Jane. Ducky, this is Jane." Pen turned to her. "Ducky's invited us to join him at his table, where Ruth is. Are you up for it?"

She certainly wasn't going to drag Jane over if she wasn't feeling well.

"I'm fine," Jane said, perking up at the sound of Ruth's name.

"Well, then."

The two women rose, and Pen had to wrap an arm around Jane just to keep her steady. She really was a duckling when it came to alcohol. Pen would be sure to remember that in the future. No more going on a toot for Jane Pugley.

Ruth was the first to acknowledge her reappearance at their table.

"Well, if it isn't Ducky with Detective Banks. Don't tell me she's lassoed you into the case of the missing body?"

"What's this about a body?" Lulu asked, playing her role perfectly.

"Let's not start that nonsense up again," Calvin grumbled.

"I agree," Mona said, giving Penelope a dark look. "It was horrid enough living through it last night."

"It seems I interrupted your conversation, Ruth. You and, ah...?" She gave Lulu a questioning look.

"Lulu Simmons," her friend replied with a gracious smile. "And Ruthie here was just telling me she's about to land in a pile of kale."

"That certainly wasn't meant for everyone's ears," Ruth said, twisting her lips with irritation.

This was certainly interesting news. Was it related to this dead woman somehow?

"I vote for murder and missing bodies. Talk of money is so gauche," Georgie said with distasteful glee.

"At least we don't have to worry about you nearly causing a dead body yourself playing a drunken game of darts with that silly knife of yours," Thomas said. "Whoever stole it did us all a favor."

"It wasn't a silly knife," Georgie protested with a frown. "It was a handsome little devil, fit for a king. An heirloom in fact."

"It *was* a lovely knife, Georgie," Ruth agreed, which only made Thomas scowl. She was quite the troublemaker.

"Isn't this supposed to be a congress?" Calvin protested. "I need to brush up on my Constitutional Law before the Bar."

"Bah, who cares about the establishment clause? I say we focus on criminal law instead." Georgie gave Pen a wink. "Surely Alfie will side with me on this, that's his bailiwick."

"I agree with Georgie," Ruth announced. "Let's discuss this dead body you found, Penelope. I think it's worth investigating. After all, if one of the Whitleys supposedly killed a woman last night it certainly couldn't have been me."

Pen wondered if her sudden enthusiasm was to keep from talking about this pile of kale she'd been discussing with Lulu.

Ruth fell back against Calvin and threw her arms around his neck, staring up at him. "As Cal can attest to, I was, *ahem*, otherwise occupied that night."

"Are you sure it wasn't Georgie you were with?" Thomas said, looking rather put out. He truly was screwy for the girl.

"Oh, I don't know, I suppose it could have been," she

sassed, giving him a particularly taunting grin that had him frowning even more.

"Couldn't have been me," Georgie said. "I had a preordained meeting with ma*mah* and pa*pah*. One does have to sing for their dinner on occasion. Spent the night at their place rather than face the rain."

So Ruth was with Calvin last night. As such, she couldn't have been the one Pen had seen slap the woman—and then kill her.

"So let's explore the other members of my family," Ruth continued, sporting a studious look.

"Not very big on family loyalty, it would seem," George commented.

"Being that none of us have ever met your family or even been to your home, perhaps there's a reason for that," Cal surmised.

"Indeed there is," Ruth confirmed. "Dullards, bluenoses, and tomcats, the lot of them. Still, if one of my siblings killed someone, they deserve to be punished, if only for tainting the Whitley name."

"Which of your siblings do you think could have done it?" Penelope boldly asked.

"Oh dear," Jane muttered next to her. She timidly reached out for the nearest glass filled with something golden to take a sip.

"She wasn't being serious, Pen," Ducky said with a nervous laugh.

"Horsefeathers, I was being perfectly serious," Ruth scoffed. "Let's start with my oldest brother William. He is, of course, above reproach. Did everything he was supposed to do in exactly the right way, even going so far as to marry a fellow ginger. And when father became ill, he stepped right into his shoes as the *pater familias*—or perhaps dictator is a better term, the way he tries to control us all. And yet, Daddy has yet to give him the keys to the financial kingdom. Even while on his sickbed he maintains control of the family business."

"Sounds as controlling as my own dear *papah*," Mona said with a light laugh.

"Oh love, your father wasn't nearly that bad," Ducky said.

"Well, mine was, as you well know, Ducky. William might as well be his twin," Ruth said.

"Wills *was* always a bit of a stuffed shirt," Ducky concurred. "Always barking at Andrew and me to stop horsing around."

Ruth laughed. "Ah yes, Andrew, completely rudderless and more than happy to spend his time with showgirls, flappers, artists, models, and other women of ill repute. The family ne'er-do-well."

"I thought that was you, Ruthie," Calvin said with a grin.

"No, I'm the—" She tilted her head in thought. "—how did my father put it? Ah yes, the 'flighty, wanton jezebel whose only success in life will come from embarrassing the Whitley name.'"

Everyone at the table laughed. Even Jane, which meant she was particularly ossified. Pen managed a smile, just to keep Ruth talking. Georgie was right, she didn't seem to have much family loyalty. She obviously butted heads with her father and oldest brother. Andrew, she seemed at worst indifferent towards. As for Tallulah—

"No, I'm nothing like perfect, beautiful Tallulah who *never puts a foot wrong*," Ruth sang while rolling her eyes. "It was inevitable she'd be the favorite and the prettiest. She was blessed with the unique and lovely name Tallulah, how could she not be? Meanwhile, I got stuck with plain, boring Ruth."

"I was positively dizzy for her when I was younger," Ducky said with a grin.

"Ducky," Mona protested with a pout.

"Not to worry, darling, I now only have eyes for you."

"Don't be too sore, Mona. Everyone loves Tallulah. Even our cantankerous father, who despises everyone. The apple of his eye, at least until she ran off to Chicago with a piano player."

"*No!*" Ducky said, leaning in with interest. "She could have had anyone, and she picked a man who tickles the ivories?"

"Indeed. Of course, when dear *pater* offered him enough money, he was more than happy to tickle his way out of her life. Just as he predicted, she came running back home, tail tucked between her legs."

So Tallulah had actually once put a foot wrong, at least in the eyes of her father. No wonder she had seemed so nervous and defeated when Pen saw her.

"And there you have it, the four Whitley children. Anything else you'd like to know, Detective Banks?"

Nothing Ruth had said about her family provided a clear-cut motive for murder. But she knew what might.

"What's this about money that you're coming into?"

Ruth's casually amused demeanor faded. "If you must know, father is dying, which means all of us are set to inherit."

"Including your cousin?"

Ruth laughed. "Yes, but before you start thinking motive, it's only *because* of her we're getting equal shares. Daddy is most likely cutting us all out of the will."

Pen blinked in surprise at that confession.

"OH yes, we're pretty sure dear Susan is getting the lion's share, if not all of it. *However*, she has promised to divide it all equally."

"Are you sure?" Pen challenged.

Ruth just smirked. "Even if she doesn't, if she dies before he does, he probably has a clause that instructs his attorney to set fire to it all rather than give us a cent. He's all but threatened as much often enough. At least with her alive, we have a hope of getting equal shares of a fortune that will very likely be almost a million. So why would any of us kill her?"

"I do believe that cancels out your theory of murder, Pen," Ducky said with a laugh, holding up his glass. The law students and Mona joined him, as though a sudden wind had lifted their sails.

Pen's own sail sagged in response. This murder was becoming more mysterious with each passing moment.

CHAPTER SIXTEEN

"I THINK IT'S TIME I HELPED MY FRIEND HOME," Penelope announced. It was probably only an hour or so until sunrise, and she needed to be at Penn Station to meet the real—or fake?—Susan Bennett that morning.

"It's definitely curtains for yours truly, as well," Lulu said.

"I'd be willing to offer a ride wherever you need to go," Pen said under the guise that she was just being generous to a new acquaintance.

"I'll go with you three," Alfie said. "It's probably not safe for you to walk alone in this area right now."

"Ho, ho, Alfie, you sly tomcat you!" Georgie teased with a grin. "Just who do you think you're fooling? Three dames for the night? Even I wouldn't be that ambitious."

Alfie met that bit of ribbing with a dry expression and didn't bother responding as he stood.

Pen gathered Jane from her chair. She could see that Benny was still preoccupied with his new friends. When he met her eye he silently indicated that they should go on without him.

Outside, the street was quiet in a way that was indeed rather ominous. Pen was glad Alfie had decided to join them. Although he looked like the clerkish type he was taller than any of them and had a certain self-assuredness in the way he carried himself.

Jane was still only half functional and Alfie took on the burden of handling most of her weight, which was admittedly not too cumbersome. At this point, she was nothing more than a rag doll.

"If you're hoping for a taxi in this part of town it's going to be rather difficult to find one," he said. "They tend to avoid this area."

"I have a car waiting near Washington Square Park," Penelope replied.

"In which case, I should probably just carry your friend," Alfie said easily picking Jane up into his arms like a child. She instinctively draped her arms around his neck and her head lolled onto the crook of it. Alfred swallowed hard and shifted to secure her more firmly in his arms.

Penelope grinned at his little act of chivalry. On the other side of him, she caught Lulu doing the same. Still, while she had him, she figured she might as well use him for information despite his stated unwillingness to help her "entrap" any of the Whitley family.

"So all of you and your friends live right around Washington Square Park? That must be awfully convenient to the law school. I suppose it also offers a nice view of the park itself."

"I'm not blessed with a view of the park. That would be George and Calvin. Calvin and Thomas live in the same building, the one they showed you earlier today. That's how they became friends, but only Cal has a view of the park. Georgie lives on the east side of the park in some former factory building. He likes to pretend his family doesn't have money."

"So which of them is Ruth actually involved with?" Lulu asked.

"I don't think she's serious about any of them, and the feeling is mutual, except in the case of Thomas perhaps. Strictly one-sided though."

"How did they all meet?"

Alfie shrugged, which caused Jane to moan and cling tighter to him. "We all usually went to the park during breaks between classes. Ruth goes to Washington Square College so she was often there as well. Georgie was the first to notice her, I believe. But he notices any attractive girl and seems to have a knack for attracting those who might be just as inclined for a bit of a lark as he is. Ruth seemed more interested in Calvin at first. I suspect he was originally only interested in her because she lives on The Row. Thomas was hooked from the beginning. She used it to her advantage bouncing around from one to the other to spark a bit of jealousy, or maybe just controversy and drama. She seems to enjoy that. Calvin is nothing if not competitive. Georgie likes to tease, especially easy targets like Thomas. There used to be a fifth in our group, Barry Henderson, smarter than all of us combined. He had her figured out from the beginning and tried to warn Thomas off her, to no avail obviously. At any rate, Barry...well, he's no longer a part of the group. Long story."

"So Ruth hasn't managed to catch your eye?" Pen asked mostly teasing.

"I don't judge her, but I have very little interest in frivolous women."

"Does Ruth often spend the night with Calvin, or I suppose Georgie or Thomas?"

Alfie sighed. "I know what you're doing, Penelope. While I hate to see a murderer go unpunished, I really don't feel comfortable being used for information, especially when it comes to my friends and acquaintances."

"If Ruth was with Calvin all night, then I doubt it was she who committed the murder. But a murder was committed all the same, and the police don't seem too enthusiastic about finding a perpetrator."

He turned to her with an eyebrow arched. "Because there was no body to be found?"

"Correct. But I know for a fact there *was* a body even if I have no idea where it might be now."

He sighed again. "I suppose I can help you with the evidentiary aspect of the crime. Unless the perpetrator had a vehicle of some sort to cart her away there are only so many places she could be. Living in the surrounding area, I do know that a few of the buildings are empty and abandoned. However, most of those spaces have been taken up by squatters, usually artists or perhaps an immigrant family. This city is becoming increasingly expensive, particularly this part of town, so there's something to be said for not having to pay for housing. With all this new development, even that's becoming a rare commodity. Around here, there are so many places no one would bother looking, buildings set for demolition to be turned into luxury apartments, and old factories that NYU plans on buying up to extend the campus. Too many to count really. However, if the perpetrator is smart, by now the body is in the Hudson River."

Penelope had to agree with him. By now the body was probably at the bottom of the Hudson River, which was the closest to Greenwich Village. If only someone would inquire about her, at least then they would have a name.

From there she could somehow find a connection to the Whitleys.

They found Leonard parked on the south side of the park. He was under a streetlamp, leaning against the hood reading a book.

"I see George is not the only one with money," Alfred remarked, noting the Rolls Royce.

"A gift from a family friend," Pen said blithely. Lulu chuckled on the other side of Alfie.

He tried to gently set Jane down, and she briefly clung to him before letting go with another moan. Pen didn't envy the hangover she'd have in the morning. After Leonard opened the door for them, Lulu took a hold of Jane and helped her inside.

Pen turned to Alfie with a grateful smile. "Thank you for escorting us to the car. It was nice meeting you today, or at this point, I suppose it was yesterday."

"You too, Penelope. It's always interesting meeting new people, and you seem...fascinating. I do wish you luck in solving your murder."

"And I wish you luck in your legal career," Pen said in return. She reached into her purse and pulled out one of the business cards she always carried with her. "If you ever need the services of an investigator for one of your clients feel free to stop by my office or call. My rates are particularly low to help those in need. Something tells me you're similarly an ally for the marginalized classes."

"On that, you seem to have me pegged," he said with a tired smile as he took the card. "I suppose I'll bid you goodnight."

Penelope joined Lulu and Jane in the backseat of the car. As Leonard started up the engine she turned to her friend. "Did you learn anything else besides the fact that Ruth is about to land in a pile of kale?"

"It was hard enough getting that much out of her. All she wanted to talk about was what it was like to sing it for a living. I think your girl's got aspirations on being some kind of artist."

"In which case, a pile of kale would come in handy. I doubt either her father or older brother would support that kind of career."

"A motive for murder?" Lulu posed.

Pen thought about it. "If the amount is really about a million and her cousin has promised a fifth of that, I don't see it. In fact, if that's the case, I don't see a motive for any of the Whitleys."

"Maybe she was lying?"

"Perhaps," Penelope mused. "I suppose there's one way to know for sure."

"What's that?"

"I plan on meeting this second Susan Bennett at the station."

CHAPTER SEVENTEEN

Having given both Leonard and poor Jane the day off after last night's activities, Penelope took a taxi by herself to Penn Station the next morning. Despite getting only a few hours of sleep, she was surprisingly spry. Perhaps it was her eagerness to meet—the real or fake—Susan Bennett and finally get some answers.

By 10:00 she was in the upper concourse nearest to where the train from Cleveland, originating in Chicago, let out.

But she wasn't the only one.

"Miss Banks," Detective Prescott greeted with a wry smile as he noticed her and approached. "I thought I might find you here."

"Don't tell me it's a crime to wait in the train station. And since there's no official police investigation to be had, you can't even accuse me of interfering."

"I suppose in this instance you do have a point.".

"Which begs the question of why *you're* here?"

"It's in the interest of the New York Police Department

to ensure the safety of any visitors to our city. Something tells me Miss Bennett might benefit from my presence." His eyes darted past her shoulder and landed on someone. Pen turned around to see William stalking their way with a firm set to his mouth.

"What the hell are you two doing here?" he demanded.

"Making sure Miss Bennett is actually alive," Penelope answered before Detective Prescott could.

"As I stated yesterday, my cousin *is* very much alive, as you'll soon find out. However, I would prefer that she not be alarmed by this nonsense about a murder, thank you very much."

"I, on the other hand, think it's very much in her best interest to be aware that there's someone going around murdering redheaded women who happened to have spent time in your home," Penelope retorted.

"Really, detective," William said in exasperation, turning his attention to the man standing next to Penelope. "Surely there's some sort of law about harassing people with made-up lies and accusations."

"None that I can think of at the moment. But I do understand your concern, Mr. Whitley. I'm only here to ensure that the woman you're meeting is in fact Miss Susan Bennett, as you claim."

"But how do we know it's the *real* Susan Bennett?" Penelope protested.

"I think I know my own cousin," William said in a testy voice. "But if you're looking for proof, she'll be bringing a letter from my father's attorney with her, a Mr. Henry Willis. I can provide you with his information. He'll be more than happy to confirm. Perhaps then we can end this nonsense of murders and missing bodies."

"That would be helpful," Detective Prescott said diplomatically.

Penelope remained silent. William was certainly good at covering for all eventualities. It seemed more and more likely that this woman they were there to meet was in fact the real Susan Bennett.

In which case who was the woman Pen had seen two nights ago?

The first wave of travelers entered the concourse and all three of them turned to scan the faces. All Penelope had to go on was red hair, which was made all the more difficult by the modern trend of bobs and shingles, mostly hidden underneath hats. She supposed that was one benefit of having William there with them. He presumably knew what his own cousin would look like.

The eyes of a young woman who had been searching for someone finally landed firmly on William and widened. Penelope studied her as she quickly approached them.

Susan Bennett wasn't at all what she had expected. The dead woman she had seen by the fountain had been dressed as though going to, or coming back from a party. Her dress and shoes had been modern and showy, just as her hair had been, despite how disheveled everything had been at the time.

This woman was pretty in an understated way, with an open face and wide, mesmerizing gray eyes that looked out at the world in pleasant wonder. Her hair was most definitely Whitley red, almost matching that of the woman Pen had seen by the fountain, if it hadn't been darkened by the rain. But this Susan's was long rather than bobbed, and gathered in a soft bun at the nape of her neck, a hairstyle that reminded Penelope of Jane. She wore an old-fashioned, wide-brimmed hat that even during its time, about ten years ago, hadn't been all that fashionable. Her dress was equally plain, a simple, loose, white shift dress with tiny, faded flowers, and nearly reached her ankles.

The one thing that stood out was a thin, gold chain around her neck with a trinket on it...in the shape of a music note. Yet another thing the two women had in common.

Penelope felt instantly charmed by how open and genuine her smile was. Still, she wasn't about to be swayed by it. Pen had been fooled by charm and innocence one too many times before.

"Susan," William said in a brisk tone. "Welcome to New York."

"Cousin William," she said far more pleasantly. "It's so nice to finally meet you."

"Yes, yes," he said, obviously not comfortable with even this tiny show of familiarity. "We should get you back home. I'm sure you're tired from your journey." He took hold of her worn suitcase.

"Oh, I'm quite fine. I had a pleasant little nap on the ride in, and it is rather thrilling to be in New York for the first time." Her eyes landed with a questioning look on Penelope and Detective Prescott.

"Your cousin said that you had a letter from the family attorney?" Pen asked, not caring that both the men next to her seemed perturbed by the question asked without preamble.

"Are you from Mr. Willis's office? Yes, I brought the letter. Did he need it for some reason? I had planned on meeting with him, as per his request. I didn't realize he needed to see me quite this urgently."

"She is most certainly *not* from Mr. Willis's office,"

William said. "She is an *interloper* intent on causing trouble. Please ignore her, Susan."

"I on the other hand am a New York police detective, and I would appreciate seeing this letter," Detective Prescott said.

"A detective?" Susan asked, her eyes growing wide. "Is there some problem?"

"None at all," he said, stopping Penelope just as she opened her mouth to speak. He gave her a quick warning look before smiling at Susan. "It's just that there has been someone who may have been trying to impersonate you, and we need to make sure you are the real Susan Bennett."

William quietly exhaled with impatience.

"Someone trying to impersonate me?" Susan said with a small laugh, tinged with both humor and uncertainty. "Why on earth would anyone want to do that?"

"Money?" Penelope blurted out. She continued on, once again ignoring the looks from William and Detective Prescott. "You are named in Mr. Whitley's will, correct?"

"So I've been told. But surely the only people who would even know about that, other than myself, are my uncle, my cousins, and Mr. Willis." She turned to William for confirmation.

"Is that so?" Penelope said, also turning her attention to William with a pointed look.

"That's hardly the case," he said, testy once again. "Heaven knows our father's ailing health is no secret, neither is his wealth. And who knows which of my siblings have been blabbing to their friends about a cousin coming to visit."

"Frankly, I'd like to clear all of this up. The letter is in my suitcase." Susan gestured to the piece of luggage in William's hand. He seemed reluctant to cooperate, but when his eyes fell on Detective Prescott, he sighed and walked over to one of the benches and set it down.

Susan bent over and unlatched it. The envelope sat on top of what looked like more plain, homespun dresses. It was quite obvious that whatever wealth Mr. Whitley had amassed hadn't trickled to her branch of the family tree.

"Here you are, detective," she said, holding the envelope out to him.

Penelope scanned the front of it along with Detective Prescott. The "From" area was indeed a Mr. Henry Willis with an address on Lexington Avenue, and the "To" area included a Miss Susan Bennett, but with an address in a town called Monroeville, not Cleveland.

"Would you like to read the contents?"

"Yes."

"No."

Penelope and Detective Prescott both spoke at the same time, leaving Susan perfectly perplexed. "It's really nothing more than a confirmation that my uncle has included me in his will and a request to meet with him at his office while I'm here in New York."

She began pulling the letter out for them.

"That won't be necessary, Miss Bennett," Detective Prescott assured her, giving Penelope a quick look of disapproval. "With this, I'm happy to take you at your word, and that of Mr. Whitley's, that you are who you claim to be."

Susan gave another small nervous laugh as she placed the letter back on top of her clothes. She closed the suitcase and re-latched it. William was quick to pick it back up.

"I trust this puts an end to this?" William said, reserving most of his contempt for Penelope.

"Yes, it does," Detective Prescott said before Penelope

could respond. "I'm sorry for the trouble, Miss Bennett. Welcome to New York."

"Thank you, detective," William said, again in a terse voice. He cast one final dark look Penelope's way before leading a still perfectly bewildered Susan Bennett away.

"You aren't going to leave it at that are you?"

"I'm not sure what else you expect, Miss Banks."

"Miss Banks is it? Does that mean you're opening an official line of inquiry? Are we going back to being nothing more than detective and New York resident? And after all we've been through together." She pouted for effect.

"*Penelope*," he said with a subtle tug at the corners of his lips. "Please tell me what it is you expect of me?"

"We should have at least warned her about the murder, *Richard*."

"And what good would that do other than cause her unnecessary worry? At this point, every member of the Whitley family knows that there is a cloud of suspicion over them with regard to a potential dead woman. A woman who not only resembles *that* Susan Bennett, but also went by the same name. I hardly think they're likely to kill another one so soon after the fact."

"And if they do? Her death will be on you, detective."

"And I'm willing to accept that blame, if indeed it does happen. In the meantime, there is something I think we *can* do, if you're not too upset with me that is?"

Penelope blinked in surprise. It was so rare for Detective Prescott to ask her to join him in any of his investigative efforts, she wasn't sure if she had heard correctly.

"Me? What is it you need me for?"

"Your brain."

"My brain?"

"Specifically your memory. I take it you remember what the writing on the envelope looked like?

"Of course, every detail."

"Fine then, let's confirm, shall we?"

He hooked his arm out and Penelope found herself slightly pleased, though also still perturbed with him. All the same, she hooked her arm through his and allowed him to escort her out of Penn Station.

CHAPTER EIGHTEEN

HENRY WILLIS'S LAW PRACTICE WAS LOCATED ON 25TH and Lexington in a tidy, attractive stone building. His office was on the second floor behind a door with the standard beveled glass that had "Law Offices of Henry Willis" painted in gold on the outside.

Penelope and Detective Prescott were greeted by a sensible-looking woman in her fifties, who seemed as though she had been entrenched in this office since it first opened. She greeted the two of them with a welcoming but no-nonsense smile, as though she was happy to greet new clients but didn't want her time wasted with nonsense.

"Good morning, how can I help you?"

Penelope was more than happy to allow Detective Prescott to use his authority to get them past this particular guard dog.

"I'm Detective Prescott and this is my..." He turned to Penelope and arched an eyebrow. "My assistant, Miss Banks."

"I see," the woman said not at all impressed, but still

offering a pleasant enough smile. "And again, how can I help you?"

"We need to commandeer about five minutes of Mr. Willis's time if that's possible?"

Her eyes narrowed slightly, "I see, and may I ask as to what this is regarding?"

"We simply need to confirm some evidence in a case," Detective Prescott said, then quickly added, "Neither he nor any of his clients are in trouble, I can assure you."

"Well, that's certainly a relief," she said with a pat smile. She rose and gestured towards the leather couch opposite her. "Please have a seat while I see if Mr. Willis is available."

When she disappeared behind a door to the right of her desk Detective Prescott turned to Penelope. "I wonder if it would have any impact at all if I were to ask you to allow me to do the talking."

"I'm just happy that you've decided to take this case seriously. By all means detective, the stage is yours."

"There's a refreshing change from the usual."

"You make it seem as though I'm as nefarious as Iago from *Othello*. I don't know why you constantly see me as an adversary. Surely you realize by now that we work well together, even with my *meddlesome* nature."

"I can't deny you certainly have your talents...and charms," he said with a subtle smile.

Penelope absently pushed her hair back behind her cloche hat. It was an irksome habit she had on the rare occasions Richard Prescott made her feel flustered. Usually, she had a bit of fun with their banter and the way he reacted to her flirtations, but then there were moments when he left her positively befuddled.

This particular moment was interrupted by the door opening.

"Mr. Willis is able to meet with you for a brief moment," his secretary said.

The two of them rose and walked past her into a large office that offered a view of the street below. It had stately wood paneling that gave the impression of reliability most people were looking for in an attorney. The man who stood up to greet them from behind a large oak desk was the same, white-haired with a mustache and a well-tailored three-piece suit. His expression was surprisingly cheerful, which contrasted with the suspicious nature of his secretary.

"Good morning. Please, please have a seat," he said in a tone to match the pleasant look on his face as he gestured to the two chairs opposite him behind the desk.

Penelope and Detective Prescott took a seat. He did the same, resting back with his fingers interlaced over his stomach. He peered at them with some amusement in his eyes.

"I must admit you've certainly sparked my curiosity, Detective Prescott, and of course your lovely assistant." He glanced at Penelope and his mouth twitched. "I don't think that I've ever seen a police detective working with a female assistant. It makes me all the more intrigued. What is this evidence you need help with?"

"Nothing that should take up too much of your time, just a bit of clarification regarding a client of yours."

His pleasant expression faded. "Is that so?"

"The Whitley family, I believe you represent them?"

Mr. Willis studied them for a moment. "As you are probably aware, detective, the dictates of my profession require that I maintain strict confidentiality. Technically, even answering such a question might be a violation."

"If it reassures you, the answer might be in your client's

best interest. We're trying to investigate a case of fraud. Furthermore, my *real* inquiry is regarding a Susan Bennett. Would she be a client of yours as well?"

Mr. Willis's mouth hitched up on one side, as though he found the question rather brash. "You should have been an attorney, Detective Prescott, you seem to have a knack for loopholes. No, Miss Bennett is not a client of mine."

"I have no interest in tricking you into violating your ethical legal obligations, Mr. Willis. I simply need to know if you sent a letter to Miss Bennett, to what address it was sent, and if we could have a sample of your handwriting to compare with the writing on the envelope that we were shown. That is all."

Mr. Willis paused yet again, studying them both before coming to a decision. "I do believe that may fall within the purview of my ethical mandates. Yes, I did send a letter to Miss Bennett requesting a meeting with her. What that meeting is about is, of course, a matter of confidentiality."

"Of course."

"My secretary, Mrs. Damond will have her full address on file. I should point out that it would also be her handwriting on the envelope. I don't typically waste my time on such administrative matters. I'll instruct her to provide both of those things."

"Thank you, Mr. Willis."

"May I ask what this business regarding fraud is?" he asked before they could stand to leave.

"There is a possibility that someone may have been trying to impersonate Susan Bennett."

"Is that so?" he asked, his brow rising again. There was no longer a cheerful spark in his blue eyes, which became suddenly steely.

"I don't suppose you've met Miss Bennett in person?" Detective Prescott asked.

"No, no, nor do I know what she looks like, I'm afraid. But...this is a curious business, I must say, and rather suspicious on top of that."

"It usually is in the case of fraud. You wouldn't be able to offer anything to illuminate your concerns?"

"Once again, my hands are tied, detective," he said with a rueful smile. "But...I will say that I specialize in estate law, wills and trusts, and such. From there you can most likely surmise what issues might arise. People think criminal law is treacherous territory," he chuckled. "Thugs and ruffians have nothing on your average upstanding citizen when an estate is at issue. I've seen the most law-abiding citizen turn into the most dastardly sort over something as minor as a single rare coin or heirloom jewelry. Now, imagine what a potentially much more vast amount might bring out in people. The Bible had it right, the love of money is the root of evil."

"Are you saying that there was contention among the Whitleys over the amount being left in their father's will?" Penelope asked.

Mr. Willis's gaze pierced her. "I'm saying no such thing, young lady. Not officially."

Penelope ignored the exasperated look Detective Prescott gave her.

"However," Mr. Willis continued. "Being that you've brought up the subject of contention, I suppose it wouldn't violate any privileges for me to say that Phillip Whitley is a contemptible man, to put it bluntly. A mean sort of individual, who enjoys causing angst simply for the sake of it. I don't envy his children. I also don't believe in terminating a relationship with a client once I've taken them on, which is the only reason I am still Mr. Whitley's attorney. However, I will say, this is one professional relationship I look forward to ceasing, whenever it is that God sees fit. Apparently, that won't be long now. May he Rest In Peace, of course."

He noted the looks of shock on their faces at how nakedly honest he was being.

"I know, I know, one shouldn't speak ill of the soon-to-be-dead, or their own clients I suppose, but if you ever have the misfortune of meeting the man, you'll understand why I speak so freely and critically about him. Neither Simon Legree nor Ebenezer Scrooge has anything on Phillip Whitley."

"Would that have been reflected in his will?" Penelope risked asking.

Once again she was met with a hard gaze from Mr. Willis. "I suppose I can't fault you for pressing your luck, but I'm no fool...Miss Banks was it? Would that be one Penelope Banks?"

Pen sat up straighter, wondering how he knew.

He chuckled. "Please, the estate Agnes Sterling left certainly made the circuit within estate law circles. I even met the woman a time or two, and I recognize you, though you probably don't remember meeting me so long ago." He gave her a scrutinizing look. "I can see why she left the bulk of everything to you. She seemed the sort to approve of women who overstepped their boundaries. That wasn't a criticism, mind you. All the same, I have a feeling any more time in your presence might be occupationally hazardous for me. I'm well aware of your successes in detective work. As such, I do believe our brief moment of time is up. I'll have Mrs. Damond provide you with the address and sample of her handwriting."

By way of dismissal, he stood up and gave a slight bow.

Pen was satisfied with the interview. She had learned quite a bit, which rounded out the picture she had of the Whitley family. Plus, they were about to get exactly what they had come for.

Mrs. Damond provided the address and handwriting sample as instructed. Both perfectly matched what Penelope remembered from the envelope, complete with the fat, rounded loops in the scripted capital S and B of Susan Bennett's name. The real tell-tale sign was the way she combined the two Ts at the end of her last name, one strike swishing down at the end as it crossed both letters.

"Yes, both are the same," Penelope confirmed.

They thanked her and Mr. Willis and left.

Once outside, Penelope turned to him. "I thought it was worth the risk to press him as much as I could. I know you're upset with me but—"

"Nonsense, Or should I say Pineapples?"

"It's applesauce," Pen said, twisting her lips. "Pineapples is to be used when you find yourself vexed with me. Which, to be honest, I thought you might be."

"The meeting went as I'd hoped. I knew you would press him for questions that he wouldn't be allowed to answer. Coming from me they might have been seen as a bit too authoritative, coming from you it would simply be..."

"Meddlesome," Penelope said curtly, upset that she had been used without her knowledge.

"Now you have some idea how I feel," he said with a grin.

"At least we got more than we anticipated. I suspect Phillip Whitley wasn't quite as generous in his will as Ruth let on last night."

He arched a brow. "Is there anything you would like to tell me?"

"Only if you promise not to arrest me."

"That sounds ominous."

"I may have run into her at a club, the kind that's strictly...prohibited, shall we say?"

"I see."

"The Golden Swan."

"*What*?"

"Not to worry, I had Benny and Lulu with me. And Jane if that makes you feel better."

"It doesn't," he gritted out. "You took *Jane*?"

"She wanted to go. In all fairness, it's a mistake neither of us shall make again, but think of the experience she's had!"

He sighed heavily, removing his hat to run a hand over his hair, as he always did when he was particularly frustrated.

"Are you going to scold me or do you want to hear what I learned?"

He replaced his hat and sighed again. "Tell me."

Pen told him what little she had learned last night, about Ruth expecting to get a sizable amount after her father's death, her descriptions of her family, and about her carousel of rather casual relationships with Thomas, Calvin, and George, also about Alfred's suggestion that the body may have been taken to an abandoned building. Detective Prescott agreed that by now it would have been taken somewhere it would never be found, like the river.

"Apparently she was with Calvin the night of the murder, so I suppose that's her alibi."

"But they all live right around Washington Square Park?"

"Yes, but why would he have been involved? I got the

impression that Calvin likes her well enough, but certainly not to the point of helping her commit murder."

"Still, the larger problem seems to be who this mystery woman is, and more importantly why she was killed. If she came on the train from Cleveland I doubt anyone in New York would know who she was."

"Actually," Pen said, brightening up. "There is someone."

CHAPTER NINETEEN

"So this David Cranberry gave you his telephone number?"

Penelope was tickled by Detective Prescott's jealousy, or at least that was how she chose to interpret his furrowed brow.

"I told him I would let him know if I learned anything about Susan Bennett. Well, now I know something, don't I?"

Rather than call, Detective Prescott had used the number to discover Dave Cranberry's address via the phone company.

Now they were at his apartment building located in the Bowery district. It was an older building that resembled most tenement housing, no decorative features save for those little frills each tenant had decided to add on their own. In one window box, Penelope saw a row of pretty flowers that looked awfully familiar. It also looked as though a few were missing.

Or rather, stolen.

"That *scoundrel.*"

"Pardon?" Detective Prescott asked.

She pointed to the flower box. "He stole the flowers he was bringing her that day."

"That doesn't necessarily make him a murderer."

"No man who steals flowers to give to a woman is worthy of that much goodwill. He's guilty of something, I'm sure of it."

"If we accuse him from the start he'll definitely clam up."

"Understood, detective."

They saw on the apartment listings that David Cranberry lived in Apartment 3C. The front door was propped open, so they walked in and took the stairs up.

After knocking on his door, they heard rustling on the other side and a few disgruntled noises.

"Who is it?" A muffled voice called out.

"It's Penelope Banks. The woman you met near Washington Square?

"How did you get my address?" he demanded, his voice understandably filled with surprise.

"If you could open the door, I have information about Susan Bennett."

There was a pause and she could hear him muttering to himself. "Just, ah, give me a moment."

He finally opened the door a crack. She could tell they had caught him by surprise. He'd quickly run a comb through his hair, but he was stuffing his wrinkled shirt into the waistband of his equally wrinkled pants.

He paused when he caught sight of Detective Prescott next to her.

"This is my..." Pen turned to arch a brow his way. "My assistant, Detective Prescott."

"Detective?" Dave asked with mild panic. "Is there some, uh, trouble?"

"No trouble," Pen said. "It's just that it seems there are two Susan Bennetts."

"Two." The way he said it was less of a question than an echo. He scratched his head. "So someone is going around impersonating her?"

"It's beginning to look like your version was the impersonator."

"Really?" His eyes widened, now in honest surprise. "Have you found her then?"

Penelope and Detective Prescott looked at each other.

"Perhaps it's best if we talk inside."

"My place is a bit of a mess. Let's go outside instead." He stepped out into the hallway, closing the door behind him.

"Are you hiding something?" Pen asked, suspicious.

"What?" He gave her a distracted look. "No, I just...it really is a mess in there. The maid's day off and all," he said sarcastically.

"We don't mind the mess," Detective Prescott insisted.

Dave said and exhaled a laugh. "Okay look. I'm not hiding anything for Pete's sake."

He opened the door for them, and Pen wasn't so much taken aback by the state of slovenliness as the sparseness. There wasn't even a couch to sit on. She thought back to the nice suit he had worn when she first met him. It had been made of quality clothing but dated.

So Dave was someone who was recently down on his luck. All the better to woo a soon-to-be heiress.

"Are you satisfied?" Dave insisted.

"I suppose we can go outside and talk."

He grunted and closed the door before leading them

back downstairs. Once outside, he pulled out a pack of cigarettes and lit one, using a match from a box. Pen noted that the box was from Delmonico's, which certainly didn't fit with the image of a man who couldn't afford furniture. The restaurant was barely affordable for the average person.

David Cranberry was a living contradiction.

"Can you tell me more about the woman you met on the train?"

He shrugged and exhaled. "I told you what I know. She got on in Cleveland, said she was coming here to meet her extended family."

"What did you talk about for three hours?" Pen pressed.

He gave her an irritated look. "Just things we enjoyed, books, movies, things like that."

"What books did she like?"

He paused, eyeing Pen as he took a drag from his cigarettes. "Uh, that one with...*Little Women*! That was it."

"Any others? What films did she like?"

"Listen, I don't remember everything. I just remember her," he said in exasperation.

"Odd for someone who was so smitten only a day ago. Anyone who had met you then would swear you were in love."

Now, he was angry. "Well, it seems she wasn't who she claimed to be either, was she?"

"Why don't you tell us what really happened on that train," Detective Prescott demanded.

"It went down exactly as I stated," Dave insisted. "She got on in Cleveland. A man was making advances, I stepped in, then stayed with her the entire ride here."

"And when you arrived in New York? Did anyone meet her at the station?" Pen asked.

"No, in fact, I offered to escort her, but she said no. Got in a taxi and left me there."

"A taxi, from Penn Station?"

He nodded.

If this imposter had presumably paid for her own ticket and taxi, not to mention the nice clothing she had on. She wasn't poor or humble, nothing like what the real Susan Bennett presented to the world.

"And she gave you, a perfect stranger the address?"

"I guess I have a nice smile," he said, curling his lips up around his cigarette.

Pen and Detective Prescott eyed one another, communicating silently before she turned back to face David.

"Which would make you a suspect."

His smile faded and his eyes went wide. He tore the cigarette away from his lips. "A suspect for what?"

"She was murdered the night before I met you."

"Wait a second, you're telling me she's *dead*?"

"That's what murdered usually implies. Do you have an alibi for that night?"

"Hey," he said, catching on. "No, no, you ain't putting this one on me. I just rode a train with the dame. Why would I show up the next day with flowers if I had bumped her off?"

"To make yourself look innocent of course. If this woman really was an imposter, she *might* entertain a conversation with a perfect stranger. But then to give you the address of where she was planning to commit her bit of fraud?"

"What makes you think my version was the fraudster?"

Pen allowed Detective Prescott to handle that question and instead focused on the man himself. There was something about him that was off. The suit he'd worn and the matchbox from one of the most expensive restaurants in the city, combined with this apartment and stealing flowers.

It hit her suddenly. "Which one of the Whitley's hired you?"

Having spent three years playing cards to make ends meet, Pen could read tells better than most people. Dave revealed his—a hard blink—before he quickly masked it.

"I don't know what you're talking about."

"The suit you were wearing? Where did you get it? It isn't yours, is it? It's an old one given to you perhaps? Something to make you look respectable, well-off even. As though you weren't after a woman for the money she was about to inherit?"

His jaw hardened. "It's mine."

"When did you dine at Delmonico's?" She asked, nodding toward the pocket in which he'd stored his matchbox. "How did you pay for a meal there?"

He swallowed in surprise, a brief flash of regret coloring his gaze.

"Mr. Cranberry, need I remind you this is a murder investigation?" Detective Prescott said.

He took a moment to mull that over, sucking hard on his cigarette before flicking it away in frustration.

"I didn't do anything illegal. I certainly didn't kill the dame!"

"Tell us everything," Pen said, her heartbeat quickening.

He studied them for a moment before sighing in resignation. "Okay yes, I was hired to meet her on the train and set up a little scenario where she was...encouraged to sit with me. I was only supposed to get to know her. I should have known something was wrong. She didn't act like no pastor's daughter I ever met. Usually, I gotta work a bit harder to win a dame over," he said with a grin. It quickly faded when he realized the circumstances.

"Who hired you?"

"Andrew Whitley."

Pen and Detective Prescott glanced at one another.

"How do you know him?" Pen asked.

"I'm in the theater, but...roles have been slow to come lately. Andrew goes to a lot of parties with showgirls and such, same as me. He came up to me at one and offered me this gig. Gave me money for the fare to get out to Chicago and back again, threw in the suit as well. Even took me to Delmonico's just to sweeten the deal. That's how I got the matchbox. It wasn't as though I was in a position to say no to anything that was paying real money."

"What is it he wanted you to do? Exactly."

"Like I said, just get to know her. Find out what she was coming out here to New York for. Mostly whether or not she knew how much she would be getting in that will. Maybe convince her to do the charitable thing and divvy it up among the rest of the family, or maybe just give a chunk to him," he said with a humorless chuckle.

"So he assumed or knew he wouldn't be getting anything in the will?" Pen asked.

David shrugged. "I guess so? He didn't get *that* personal with me."

"So he didn't know she was an imposter?"

"If he did he certainly didn't tell me," Dave groused.

Why go to all the trouble of hiring someone if he knew she wasn't the real Susan? On the other hand, it was all the more reason Andrew Whitely might be angry if he found out he'd wasted time and money on a woman who turned out to be a fraud.

"Listen, I told you everything I know. I had no idea the

lady wasn't the real thing. I certainly had no reason to kill her. Why would I? I had already gotten paid."

"Why did you show up at the Whitley residence?"

He gave them a guilty look. "I figured we hit it off and all. If she really was coming into money...."

"Why not hook your claws in early on?" Pen finished in a cynical voice.

He shrugged and grinned. "Ain't nothin' illegal in that."

"Did the maid really claim Susan Bennett wasn't there when you spoke with her?"

"Yeah, but I figured it was just the family trying to keep a fortune hunter away."

"So, just to be clear, you knew the address because she gave it to you, not because you already knew where Andrew lived?"

"She gave it to me, I swear."

It was apparent that Dave Cranberry thought the Susan Bennett he was wooing was the real one. The only problem is, so did Andrew Whitley, who should have known better.

"Thank you for your time, Mr. Cranberry. We'll be in touch if we need anything more," Detective Prescott said, when it was obvious they had nothing more to ask.

"Yeah," Dave said, not looking happy as he went back inside.

"It looks like Andrew Whitley is our next person of interest," Detective Prescott said.

CHAPTER TWENTY

PENELOPE AND DETECTIVE PRESCOTT WERE BACK NEAR Washington Square, headed to the Whitley residence to speak with Andrew. It was another lovely day and the park was crowded that afternoon, especially now that the sogginess from the rain had evaporated.

Pen smiled as the sound of children's laughter filled the air. She looked over to see several of them, each probably no more than five, chasing each other near the fountain. On the other side, she could see the familiar group of law students once again. Yes, the park was an attractive distraction, but Pen briefly wondered how they got any studying done with all these smoking and debating breaks. Though it seemed only Calvin and Georgie were the smokers in the group. The latter was animated, as usual, regaling them with some story or perhaps another fascinating case in the news. Cal stood next to him, idly smoking and staring off with his brow furrowed in deep thought. Thomas and Alfred had their backs to her so she couldn't read their expressions.

Before they reached the Whitley home, the door opened and Tallulah walked out. She was almost as pretty as the day was, wearing nothing more than a simple white frock and a sun hat. She stopped to look out at the park, staring at the children at play near the fountain, with a small, bitter frown on her face. Perhaps she was thinking of the children she'd never have with her piano player. Penelope felt a pang of sympathy hit her.

Tallulah must have sensed their approach because she turned to them, a flash of alarm in her eyes. Penelope remembered how skittish she had been during their first interaction so she plastered a reassuring smile on her face.

"Miss Whitley," Detective Prescott greeted.

"Detective, and...Miss Banks, was it?"

"Penelope, please," she said graciously.

"Was there something more you needed?" Tallulah asked with an anxious look on her face.

"We've actually come to talk to your brother Andrew. Is he in?"

"Andrew?" Now a confused expression colored her features.

"Yes."

"I, um, I'm afraid not, detective. I suppose he's out with one of his theater or art friends. You might check back tonight, but he usually spends most nights at one party or another especially as the weekend nears."

"A party you say?" Penelope asked brightening up.

Tallulah's eyelashes fluttered her way. "At least I assume so. One of the artists in those lofts hosts one almost nightly, it seems." She waved a hand toward the east side of the park, where Georgie lived. A wistful smile whispered across her lips. "Andrew and Ruth, the two wayward younger Whitley children, but at least they get to enjoy their youth."

"Yet you were prevented from marrying your piano player," Pen said sympathetically.

A flash of intense emotion came to Tallulah's face, which almost made Penelope regret mentioning him. But she hadn't ruled any of the Whitley children out as far as murder. Still, Tallulah quickly recovered.

"Father was right, there was no future for me with Reggie. Certainly not so far away from home, living in Chicago. Who would be here to take care of him now? Certainly not Ruth. Yes, there's Caroline, William's wife, but father isn't her obligation, especially being so newly wed. They're trying to start a family of their own, you know." Her mouth tightened into a bitter frown. "As such, it's my responsibility being that I'm the oldest...and still unmarried."

"You haven't thought about marrying someone else or at least entertaining the idea of a new suitor?" Pen inquired. She certainly was beautiful enough, and coming from a fine family like the Whitley's she'd have her pick.

A brief smile, tinged with bitterness or cynicism, touched Tallulah's mouth before responding. "Perhaps one day. For now, father needs me."

"Family loyalty above all else."

Tallulah stared at her, long enough to make Pen think what she had said struck some nerve. She looked as though she wanted to tell her something, then her eyes darted to the windows of her home and she seemed to think better of it.

"I really must be off. I'm only supposed to be going out to get father some more medicine. William will be expecting me back soon."

"What is it, Tallulah?"

She stared at Pen for another long moment, and she was

sure Tallulah was about to tell her. Once again, she gazed at her home and sagged, shaking her head.

"I can't," she whispered. She quickly turned and scurried off in the other direction.

Penelope and Detective Prescott watched her reach the end of the block. Before turning north onto 5th Avenue, she looked back one last time, something in her gaze longing to tell them something, then she looked away and hurried on.

"She was definitely going to tell us something."

"Yes, she was," Detective Prescott said. He took hold of Pen's hand. "Come with me."

Instead of following Tallulah east towards 5th Avenue, he led Penelope in the opposite direction.

"Where are we going?"

"We're going to head her off from the other direction without raising any suspicion, just in case a certain member of the Whitley family is watching through the windows."

They hurried down the block and then headed north. At the next street, they headed back in the direction toward where Tallulah might be. They caught her in the middle of the next block.

"Miss Whitley," Detective Prescott called out.

She spun around in surprise, her eyes wide with alarm. "What is it?"

"I had the feeling there was something you wanted to tell us. If there's anything you know, anything that might help discover who this woman is and what may have happened to her, it's important that you tell us."

"I-I really don't know anything definite. Certainly not who may have killed her." That fretful looked came to her face.

"What is it Tallulah?" Penelope asked in a gentler tone. "We're just trying to find out who this poor woman was so we can give her family some solace." She hoped that tugging at her heartstrings might do the trick.

Tallulah just seemed more agitated.

"There's no reason anyone has to know that it came from you," Detective Prescott said.

Looking suddenly overwhelmed Tallulah exhaled. "The woman, I don't know who she really is, but yes, she was at our house that night."

Although she already knew this, Penelope jerked her head back in surprise at the confession. "So why lie about it?"

"William said it was for the best. He didn't want the police pinning any murder on one of us when none of us had killed her."

"Let's start from the very beginning. Tell us everything you know about this woman and her interactions with any member of the Whitley family," Detective Prescott said.

Tallulah nodded numbly. "She arrived that day, before the night of the thunderstorm. We all thought she was really our cousin. I must admit I was a bit surprised at how...*brash* she was. But one never knows, do they? And I know a lot of young women like to act out in their youth." She blushed as though remembering her own "indiscretion." "Then...much later that night, before the storm started, I heard a commotion downstairs. I'm a light sleeper, because of father, so I think I was the only one awakened by it. It was William and this woman arguing."

That must have been the point at which the lights in the Whitley household came on while she was breaking into the arch.

"What were they arguing about?"

"I didn't understand it at first. William was accusing her

of not doing her part. I assumed it was in relation to the will."

"The will?" Detective Prescott asked.

"Yes," Tallulah said with a sigh. "All of us knew father might have been planning to give Susan everything. But we had been reassured by her very own hand that she planned on dividing it equally among all of us, no matter what the will stated. I thought he was angry about her reneging on her promise, but it didn't sound that way."

"How so?" Penelope asked.

"He said something about father not believing she was really Susan Bennett and that perhaps if she had dressed and acted more appropriately it would have been more believable. Then..." She paused again, nibbling her bottom lip as though wondering if she should continue. Penelope and Detective Prescott waited. "Then, William said she could keep the money as it was the last she would be getting from him, and that she had to leave the house that instant and never darken our doorway again."

"So, he had paid her?" Penelope confirmed.

"That's what it sounded like. But why would he pay our cousin to come out to New York? That's when I realized she probably wasn't the real Susan Bennett. She all but confirmed it with her response. She threatened to reveal that he had paid her to act as our cousin and that if he didn't pay her more, a *lot* more, she would not only tell the rest of the family, including father, but she would go to the police as well. That's when...he slapped her."

Penelope stood up straighter, feeling slightly justified. This confirmed everything she had either seen or suspected.

"But he didn't kill her," Tallulah was quick to say. "Of that, I'm certain. He told her that no one would believe some conniving tart over a Whitley. Yes, he may have manhandled her a bit as he led her to the door and threw her out, but she was still alive when he closed the door. I'm sure if he knew it would storm so horribly, he might not have acted so rashly."

So she had been alive when she was kicked out of the house?

"I still have no idea who that woman really was, but when you came to our house yesterday, I didn't feel there was anything that I could offer that might help you find out. I'm sorry I didn't say anything sooner."

"So, just to be clear, this woman *did* meet with your father? And according to William, your father discovered she wasn't the real Susan Bennett?"

Tallulah nodded. "That's what it sounded like."

"And then William kicked her out of the house," Penelope asked in a slightly cynical tone.

"Yes. No one who was home that night killed her."

"Except Ruth wasn't there that night," Penelope said.

Tallulah's eyelashes fluttered. "Well, yes, Ruth does have a habit of...spending the night with...friends." She pursed her lips with distaste. "But that certainly doesn't mean she killed this woman either. How would she have even known William kicked her out of the house? Or that she wasn't really our cousin?"

It did seem like it would be quite the coincidence.

"That's all I know detective, I swear."

"One more question," Penelope said. "Was she wearing a gold bracelet with a small trinket in the shape of a musical note when she was kicked out?"

A confused smile came to Tallulah's face. "No, I don't think so. In fact, I'm certain of it. I think maybe William took it back from her before throwing her out."

So it must have been William who bought the bit of

jewelry to add a note of authenticity. But their father had still not been fooled. Why not?

"Thank you, Miss Whitley, this has been very helpful," Detective Prescott said.

"I know William was a bit aggressive with her and quite angry but I can't imagine he killed her."

"So, what do you make of that?" Penelope asked Detective Prescott when Tallulah continued on with her errand.

He stroked his chin in thought. "So we have William hiring a woman to play Susan, in the hopes of what? The real Susan had already assured them she would be splitting the money equally. So that isn't a motive."

"Maybe he wanted more for himself? Just as Andrew did?"

"Unfortunately, the only way to know for sure is to ask him. And I doubt he'll be as forthcoming as his sister was. Really, I'm wondering how it is their father discovered she wasn't the real Susan."

"It could have been anything. Maybe she answered one of his questions incorrectly or—" Penelope stopped suddenly. "The eyes!"

"Eyes?"

"The real Susan's eyes are gray. According to David, his Susan's eyes were bright green. If the only thing William had to go on was a photograph, it would have been in black and white, and he wouldn't have known that her eyes were supposed to be gray, not green."

Detective Prescott nodded. "Either way the jig was up and he had to scramble to get the real Susan out here to make up for it. None of that necessarily spells murder though. I certainly don't see someone as precious as William Whitley running out in the middle of a thunderstorm to murder the woman he had just ousted from his house."

"Or dragging her away after the fact to dispose of her body."

"So that still leaves the question of who killed her?"

"Maybe it was just a random act of violence by some miscreant in the park?"

"I'd buy that except for the part about her body going missing after the fact. That's what makes this whole thing seem not so random."

"So we still have to consider who might still be willing to kill the real Susan Bennett," Penelope said.

"Which means, we need to talk to her as soon as possible."

CHAPTER TWENTY-ONE

DETECTIVE PRESCOTT AND PENELOPE RETURNED TO the Whitley home once again. The door was opened by the maid who met them with a frown of irritation. "Can I help you?"

"We're here to speak with Miss Susan Bennett."

"I'm afraid Miss Bennett is not in at the moment."

"And where might she be? This is urgent."

"She's with Mr. Whitley on an errand."

"And when might they return?"

"They didn't say as much," she said in a tone bordering on insolence.

"I'm a detective, ma'am and this is a police matter, so I would appreciate you being more forthcoming."

"I'll handle this Martha," a voice said. Caroline Whitley smoothly stepped in to replace her maid at the front door. She met the detective and Penelope with a cold smile. "Susan isn't in right now, she's with William. They've gone to the law office of my father-in-law to meet with Mr. Willis. I can assure you my brother's cousin is in no danger from us." She cast a brief withering look at Penelope. "Despite what some people might think."

"Was it William who suggested they meet with him so soon after her arrival?" Pen asked, unbothered by the evil look she received.

"Whatever the reason, neither she nor my husband are here at the moment. Perhaps she would be willing to call you once they return, *detective*." Pen noted how she had deliberately mentioned him and not her. She also seemed ready to close the door on them.

"How is your father-in-law? It's my understanding that he doesn't have long now?" She asked in what she hoped was a sufficiently sympathetic tone. Pen wouldn't have put it past the family to bump him off now that their dear cousin, who was likely set to inherit everything, was firmly in their clutches. The Susan she had met at the station seemed rather naive and impressionable.

"No, he doesn't have long to go," Caroline said in a terse voice. "Which is all the more reason this constant intrusion has been very upsetting." Without saying another word she shut the door in their face, startling both of them.

"Well, that was productive," Penelope said in a disgruntled voice.

"We may yet get what we came for," he said, looking past her shoulder.

Penelope turned around to see a taxi coming to a stop in front of the house. William and Susan stepped out. William looked perfectly vexed at their presence. Susan simply greeted them with a curious smile.

"Detective Prescott, Miss Banks, what a lovely surprise. Is there something more that you needed from me?" Susan greeted.

"As it turns out we do," Detective Prescott said. He cast a hard look William's way. "In private if you don't mind."

"Yes, she does mind, as a matter of fact. Honestly detective this intrusion into our family affairs has gone too far at this point. You've already frightened my cousin with this business about an imposter. Who knows what poison you plan on filling her head with. I'm not going anywhere."

"And does your cousin have a say at all?" Penelope asked feeling her righteousness come to a head. She hated officious men who felt it was their place to speak for women. "Or perhaps you're worried about what we might say to her?"

He gave Penelope a smug, but dark look. "If you plan on telling her about this other woman, I've already told her everything."

Penelope blinked in surprise. "You have?"

"Yes. I did hire a woman named Mary Tate to stand in for my cousin. I was worried that father might die before our real cousin had a chance to come out. I wanted to give him the final solace of making peace with his niece before he died, or at least someone he thought was his niece."

"And you didn't think this was important information to share with us when we came to visit you yesterday?" Detective Prescott asked in an angry voice.

"You were all but accusing my family of murder. I felt it wise to maintain my discretion. We do still have the right to remain silent in this country, do we not?"

Penelope couldn't hide her skepticism. "So you hiring this woman had nothing to do with you wanting more than your fair share from the will?"

"How dare you!"

"Oh applesauce, you didn't—"

Detective Prescott gently laid a restraining hand on

Penelope's arm. "We *are* still investigating the murder of this woman."

"Which I had no part in. I ousted her from the house after she tried to swindle our father and then blackmail me."

"So you sent Mary Tate out into the middle of a thunderstorm in the wee hours of the morning without any concern as to what might happen to her?" Penelope asked, incredulous.

"In my defense, it wasn't storming yet at the time."

"How altruistic of you," Pen spat.

"Yes, perhaps my cousin acted without proper consideration for Mary's welfare," Susan interjected. "He *has* expressed his regret to me."

"Indeed," William sniffed. "I acted rashly and with anger. Unfortunately, that may have led to her death. But *I* certainly wasn't the one who killed her. She was very much alive when she left."

"As such, I think it's important that I speak with Detective Prescott, don't you think, William? We should all do everything we can to help find out what may have happened to her."

"But..." William protested with alarm. He seemed to realize he was in no position to argue and sighed with impatience. "Fine then."

"Perhaps we could speak inside?" Detective Prescott said.

"Absolutely not, I must insist on that. Father is still ill!" William protested. "I don't want him inadvertently overhearing anything."

"Why don't we go to the park instead?" Susan suggested. "It's such a lovely day and I've yet to enjoy all its charms."

She really did put on a sweet and accommodating act.

On the other hand, she seemed to have no problem defying William, which was a point in her favor.

The three of them crossed the street into Washington Square Park and began strolling along one of the paths.

"Do you mind if I ask what you know about Mary's murder?" Susan asked. "It's just that I'd hate to think she was killed because someone else assumed she was me."

"I suppose I should leave that to Miss Banks," Detective Prescott said. "She's the one who witnessed everything."

"And apparently the only one," Penelope said with a tiny bit of irritation. "At least apart from the killer. It happened two nights ago. I was with some friends...enjoying the park. I saw an argument taking place through the windows of the Whitley home. Mary was slapped by someone. Apparently, that was William. Then perhaps fifteen or twenty minutes later, I saw her body right there by the fountain." She pointed toward the fountain on the other side of the road that ran through the park.

Susan's eyes followed her direction. "Oh dear, it does look so harmless and pleasant during the day doesn't it?"

"Someone placed the body on the other side. That lamppost you see, it wasn't functioning at the time. I saw her body in a flash of lightning. By the time we made it to the fountain someone had removed her body. We still have no idea where it is."

Susan was still staring at the fountain, her brow wrinkled with dismay. "How very sad. I shall be sure to pray for her soul."

Penelope's eyes darted back to Susan, wondering if she was being facetious. She really was committing to the kind and generous act. David had said she was a pastor's daughter and she was fitting into the role brilliantly, a little *too* brilliantly. In Penelope's experience, the daughters of pious men often had a tendency to rebel. Perhaps Susan was the exception?

"Can you think of any reason why anyone would want you dead?" Detective Prescott asked.

Susan gave a nervous laugh. "Heavens no. Other than my cousins and my uncle, I don't even know anyone in New York. I'd hate to think that anyone felt any animosity towards me."

"So you've *never* been to New York before?" Penelope asked.

Susan gave her a rueful smile. "I'm afraid not. My mother and my uncle were very much estranged. He didn't approve of her marrying my father, who was a simple pastor. It isn't that Uncle Phillip isn't a religious man. He just had higher aims for her. From what I gather, he was a rather controlling older brother once my grandfather died, long before I was born."

"So none of your cousins or even your uncle knew what you looked like?"

"He came to visit once when I was seven. I barely remember it. I believe he had offered some sort of ultimatum at the time that she refused. That was the last time they spoke to one another, at least in person. My mother wrote to him, though. She sent him a newspaper clipping of me when I was thirteen. I'd won a writing competition and they took my photo. I of course sent the obituaries when my parents died. But I've never met my uncle as an adult, so he wouldn't know what I look like."

If he had met her when she was seven, he would know what color her eyes were. As Penelope had surmised, that was the giveaway.

"Have you lived in Monroeville your whole life?"

"Yes, I was born and raised there."

"I'm sorry about your parents. How did they die?" Pen said, hoping she didn't sound too intrusive.

Fortunately, Susan didn't seem too bothered by the question. "My father was a bit older than my mother. He died of a heart attack. As for my mother, it was quite a surprise, a blood vessel burst in her head according to the doctor. Quite random. That's when I reached out to my uncle, I sent him the obituary. I figured despite their differences he would want to know."

Penelope met Detective Prescott's eyes, wondering if he was thinking the same thing she was.

"I hate to sound insensitive, but considering all the facts, I do need to ask. Is there anyone back in Monroeville who can confirm you are who you say you are?"

"Oh, of course," Susan said brightly. "It is a tiny town so almost anyone there can confirm it. I teach Sunday school at the church and assist at the local school. My parents didn't leave me much but I had the house, which I sold. I now room with an old family friend named Mrs. Darcy Brooks. I help her out with cooking, minor cleaning, assisting her in getting around, and such. She doesn't have anyone else, so it's a fine arrangement."

She really was the Good Samaritan, Penelope thought with yet another dose of cynicism. If indeed Susan turned out to be the angel that she was portraying, Pen would certainly take back her ungenerous thoughts about the woman. For now, she was still suspicious.

"Do you think my being from such a small town has anything to do with the murder?"

"Perhaps it has to do with the inheritance you're set to receive?" Penelope answered. She didn't believe in being circumspect. "If you're willing to enlighten us, do you mind telling us what it is Mr. Willis wanted to discuss with you?"

"There isn't much I can say that would help with your investigation. He just wanted to make sure that I was in town when my uncle died, being that I am named in the will. He couldn't say much more, being that my uncle is still alive and Mr. Willis is *his* attorney."

She was right, that didn't help very much.

"However, I suspect I know what information you're after and I think I may be able to enlighten you. Yes, I believe my uncle will be leaving me everything in the will."

"Everything? How do you know?"

"I received a letter from Uncle Phillip. I brought that with me as well. I hadn't planned on showing my cousins, but I thought it best to bring it with me all the same. It is..." She paused to consider her words. "It isn't very flattering toward them. In fact, I thought it rather mean-spirited. He made it quite clear that they didn't deserve a single nickel from him. When I received the subsequent letter from Mr. Willis, I knew what was in store."

"And did any of your cousins suspect they had been cut out of the will?"

"Even if they had, they certainly had nothing to worry about. When I wrote to say I was coming to visit, I made it quite clear that whatever was left to me, I would make sure they were treated equally if necessary."

"To whom did you make this clear?" Detective Prescott asked.

"Well, I wrote a letter directly to William. I figured since he was the oldest, he would let the others know."

Or perhaps not.

"When did you send this letter?"

"A couple of weeks ago. It was after I had received both letters. I suppose that was around the time that my uncle realized his time was short."

"And that's why you decided to come to New York? Both to visit with Mr. Willis and see your uncle?"

"Yes, well, I mean it was a mutual decision."

Once again Penelope caught Detective Prescott's eye.

"So you've met your uncle then?" Detective Prescott asked.

"Yes," Susan answered a sorrowful look coming to her face. "He's in so much pain, I do believe death would be a blessing. But he was at least coherent enough to recognize me as his niece. He recognized the music note my mother gave me when I won the writing contest. I wore it in the photo."

The photo William no doubt saw as well.

"Does it have some significance?" Penelope asked.

Susan's hand came up to the trinket and she looked down on it with a wistful smile. "My mother loved music. My father was the one to teach her the piano. She had grown up wanting to learn, but my uncle forbade it. He thought it was a frivolous endeavor. She gave this to me as sort of a symbol. It was originally on a bracelet, but it kept getting caught on things so we switched it to a necklace instead. I suppose she wanted to instill in me the idea that I should always follow my heart and my dreams."

That's probably why Mary's had been a bracelet rather than a necklace. William only had the photo to go on.

"And is there someone close to your heart back in Monroeville?" Penelope couldn't help but ask.

The way Susan's cheeks colored told her there probably was. "There is a man who sometimes walks me home from church. He owns the hardware store and occasionally helps fix things around Mrs. Brooks' house as well. I bake him banana bread or blueberry muffins in return."

How very quaint, Penelope thought to herself. It was actually rather sweet.

"It sounds like you had a wonderful upbringing out in Monroeville."

"Yes, my parents were lovely, they taught me the values of generosity, family, and more importantly forgiveness. I would like to believe my uncle regrets becoming estranged from my mother, even if he can't admit as much. I would like to think that's why he's been so generous with me, as an act of atonement perhaps? That's why it's important for me that money be evenly divided. I even had Mr. Willis draw up a contract stating as such, just so my cousins know I'm serious about it. I'd like to repair the damage that's been done in this family. Money is certainly nice, but I've learned family is more important."

"I think a lot of people might disagree with that," Penelope couldn't help but say.

Susan laughed. "There isn't much in Monroeville that money can buy. You have a lot of people lending a hand if you need it. That's what it's like in a small town. It's why I moved out of the house that was really too big for just me, and into the room with Mrs. Brooks."

"So you have no plans on moving to New York?"

"New York? Oh no! I mean it is..." She looked around at the park. "It certainly is a fascinating place to visit, but it's a bit too busy for my liking."

"Do you think we could see this letter that your uncle sent you if it's not too much of an intrusion?" Detective Prescott asked.

"I suppose that's fair, in the interest of justice."

They turned to walk back toward the Whitley home. Penelope and Detective Prescott waited outside, at the insistence of Caroline who refused to let them inside. While they waited, Penelope brought up her suspicions.

"Do you believe her, that she's the real Susan Bennett?"

"It all seems to fit. And she's given us enough information that it wouldn't be too difficult to confirm she's not the impostor. One train trip to Monroeville would certainly do the trick."

"I suppose," Penelope said with a sigh. "But she does seem awfully... good."

"Not villainous enough for your tastes?" Detective Prescott asked with a grin.

Penelope pursed her lips. "I suppose New York has made me rather cynical. Someone like that would be eaten alive here. We New York women have to be a bit more..."

"Meddlesome?"

She glared, but couldn't help smiling, for some reason itching to stick her tongue out at him like a schoolgirl. "Difficult."

He laughed.

The door opened and Susan reappeared, holding out an envelope to them. "Here you are."

Penelope quickly came to Detective Prescott's side so she could read the letter he removed and unfolded:

Susan,

I received your clipping of the obituary for my sister. I suppose this means you are now without a mother and a father. My condolences.

As your mother probably conveyed to you at some point in life, I did not approve of her choice of husband or her decision to leave her family and move to the place you call home.

I made my opinion on the matter quite clear often enough. She made her choices in life and she had to live with them.

I do not regret my decision to cut her off or cease all communication. Women who fail to live their life with any common sense or reason aren't worth my trouble. As her offspring, and potentially poisoned by the same well, I am inclined to cut a similar swath in my opinion of you. No doubt she raised you to be just as incorrigible as she was. The Bennett name is not one that I will ever accept as kin.

However, there is something to be said for not punishing the child with the sins of the mother. After all, you are still blood, even if not in name or anything resembling affection.

My own children are a disappointment, to say the least— a cloying sycophant, a senseless romantic, an irredeemable miscreant, and a wanton jezebel. I fear emboldening them with the benefit of my wealth, which I worked long and tirelessly to grow, shall see it squandered within a generation, if not before then.

I suspect you sent the obituary in the hopes that some compensation might be coming your way. Under normal circumstances, I would gladly absolve you of that notion. As it stands, you're the only relative I have left that hasn't been an abject failure in my eyes, and that is only because I have yet to meet you. This should tell you something about your cousins.

Should you see fit to visit before my imminent demise, I shan't turn you away. Though I don't envy the wrath you'll receive from my children upon my demise when they learn that I have left them nothing.

Regards,
P. Whitley.

. . .

Penelope had certain vile thoughts about the man after finishing the letter. It was one thing to have such opinions about his children, but to air them to someone who might as well be a perfect stranger? Even her own, also quite disappointed, father wouldn't have been that callous.

"Do you think that we could hold on to this letter?" Detective Prescott asked Susan. "We just want to confirm with a third party this is his handwriting."

"Of course, I understand," Susan said, her brow furring a little. "Still, I'd rather not too many people read what he wrote about my cousins."

"Of course, thank you for being so accommodating in this investigation. We won't take up any more of your time."

"As I said, anything I can do to help. I do hope you find out who did this, detective. Mary deserves justice," she said before going back inside.

"Well, she certainly wasn't wrong about the unfavorable opinion of his children. Do you think the letter is legitimate?" Pen asked as they walked away.

"I want to go back to Mr. Willis's office. He would be able to confirm whether or not this is his handwriting. Perhaps he may even be able to confirm we have the right Susan this time, now that he's met her. We also need to talk to Andrew at some point to clear up his story."

"Yes," Penelope agreed, looking down the block. "And I know just who we can talk to about where to find him."

CHAPTER TWENTY-TWO

Penelope led Detective Prescott back to another home further down on The Row. When she knocked on the front door, this one was answered by a butler who politely greeted her before asking how he could be of service.

"I'm here to see Ducky, er, Derrick Bishop. I'm Penelope Banks, one of his close friends."

"Pen, is that you?" She heard Ducky call out. He replaced the butler, dismissing him as he greeted her at the door. "What are you doing here?"

"I came to ask you about Andrew Whitley."

At the name, Ducky's eyes grew wide with worry. Then, a broad smile appeared.

"Actually, I'm glad you stopped by about that." He stepped outside, closing the door behind him as he urged them down the stairs and onto the sidewalk. "The Whitleys are family friends, and they're going through a lot right now what with their father being so ill. Honestly, this story about a body isn't doing anything for his health."

"It isn't a story, Ducky. I know what I saw."

He gave her a patronizing smile. "Are you sure? You did have quite a bit of champagne and gin, we all did."

Penelope realized he had no idea the man standing next to her was a detective. Detective Prescott had been conversing with the officers in the back of the station when the boys were freed from their cell and left, so none of them would have seen him. She wasn't about to enlighten him.

"I didn't see anything, Pen. I asked Mona and she didn't see anything either. Isn't it about time you dropped all this nonsense about a body? Has anyone even come to claim her? Has anyone found a body? Perhaps it's best to let the living go on living in peace, no?"

"Would you feel the same if it was your relative?" Penelope asked, appalled.

"Well, of course not, but then again I would be quick to claim a relative of mine if they'd gone missing."

The door opened and Mona stepped out, looking at them through eyes narrowed with suspicion. She came down and placed a protective hand on her fiancé's back. "What is this about, Ducky?"

"Just trying to get Pen here to see reason. Pointing out how futile it is to find a murder where there was none. After all, with the alcohol and the pouring rain on top of that... maybe you mistook a fallen branch or a pile of leaves for a woman's body?"

"I think I know the difference between a woman and a pile of leaves. I would hope for Mona's sake that you do as well."

"Oh just stop this now!" Mona cried, stomping her foot.

"There, there dear," Ducky said, placing an arm around her shoulders. "See what you've done, Pen?"

"I apologize for that," Mona said recovering. "It's just all so very distressing."

"I was just talking to William and he confessed that the woman I saw was in fact in his house that night. The same woman who ended up dead." She was bending the truth just a bit, but she wanted to see Ducky's reaction.

"William told you that?" Ducky seemed bewildered by the idea.

"Well with the facts presented, he didn't have much of a choice, did he?" Penelope said knowing she was being deliberately vague.

Ducky shook his head in consternation. "This doesn't make any sense. Did he agree with you that there was a body?"

"Well, he wasn't going to very well confess to murder, was he? Still, the fact remains that the woman isn't such a mystery after all. She now has a name, Mary Tate."

"That doesn't mean she was murdered," Mona protested. "After all, no one else saw the body, Pen. Not Ducky, not I, and I'm sure Walter would agree with us."

"You and Walter were inside at the time," Penelope pointed it out.

"There were windows looking down in the park in that room," Mona replied. "We would have had a view of the fountain from there and neither of us saw a body. You can ask him."

Penelope had a feeling she was being ambushed yet again. The first time had been with the Whitleys. Now, Ducky and Mona seemed to be combining forces to work against her.

"Why are you so interested in denying that there was a murder?"

Mona blinked and stood up straighter, looking indignant. Ducky just got more frustrated.

"Because this is my home, Penelope! No one likes the

idea of a murder taking place practically outside their front door. My parents are already displeased with me. Thank goodness they don't know about the fines from our little adventure up the arch. If they were to learn about a murder taking place at the same time, that would be the end."

"I would think they'd want the murderer found and brought to justice."

"Not when it's one of our own neighbors, good and decent people we've known our whole lives."

He was practically in a panic. This business about his parents made Pen think that perhaps his frivolous little adventure around Europe hadn't been received very well upon his return home.

She decided to change tactics. At the very least she could still get what she came for.

"You do make a good point. If I could talk to Andrew, I think it might clear things up for me."

Ducky blinked in surprise. "What?"

"Andrew might be able to give me information that would clear the entire Whitley family," she lied, if only to tell Ducky what he obviously wanted to hear.

"What does Andrew know?" Ducky asked suspiciously.

"I don't think it would be fair to reveal anything before I talk to him. Of course, I could just go to the police with this new information William gave me instead? I'm sure they would like to know the real name of the victim."

"I have no idea where he might be right now, Ducky confessed.

Oh well, that is unfortunate.

"However..." Ducky began and then seemed to stop himself. Mona glanced his way and gave him a look that Penelope couldn't read. "I do know of a party for some artists he invited Mona and me to tonight."

Although Penelope had her fill of parties this week, at least this one might prove fruitful.

"It's in one of the old factory buildings, it will get going around eleven he said." He gave her the exact address.

"Splendid!" Penelope said. "I look forward to seeing you there."

"Right," Ducky said, not looking at all enthused about the prospect. "Well, until then."

He threw an arm around Mona and hurried her back inside.

"Well that was certainly suspicious," Detective Prescott said, mirroring her own thoughts. "I'm almost certain they're hiding something."

"They are," Penelope said. "All the same, we at least have a time and place. So, are you up for a bohemian party tonight? Fortunately, they had no idea you're a detective. It could be our first undercover adventure together," Penelope said with a smile, actually looking forward to the idea.

Something glimmered in Detective Prescott's dark eyes. She felt that woosh of pleasure run through her.

"I suppose someone will have to keep you out of trouble."

"I might have to say the same thing for you," she said with a smirk. "I'd hate to lead you down the path of sin."

"Not to worry, Eve, my eyes were opened to the evils of the world long before you came along. Besides, I've always hated the idea of laying the blame on a woman, as the Bible seems inclined to do."

Pen suddenly gasped.

"What is it?"

She grinned up at Detective Prescott. "Mona. She may have very well given us another witness to the sins of the world...or at least one that took place that night."

CHAPTER TWENTY-THREE

Walter Adams worked at his father's insurance company. No doubt that was where he had developed such an analytical mind. Perhaps it's also what made him so risk averse. Penelope hoped that would work in her favor.

Penelope approached the receptionist. "I'm here to see Walter Adams. Junior," she quickly added, remembering that Walter was named after his father, a practice that she always thought was rather silly.

"Did you have an appointment?"

"No, but I was hoping he might have time for me. I'm an old friend...and I did have a rather urgent insurance need I thought he might be able to help me with. Perhaps you can impart that to him?"

The professional smile remained plastered on the receptionist's face as she picked up the phone and made the inquiry. After she hung up, Penelope was relieved to see her stand and ask them to follow her back into the offices.

Walter was already standing to greet them from behind his desk when they entered his small office. Still, there was a hint of worry on his face. That was understandable. He was smart enough to know that Penelope hadn't actually come to inquire about insurance.

"Thank you, Barbara, please close the door behind you."

Penelope and Detective Prescott took the two chairs across from his desk once the receptionist left. Walter remained standing for a moment, the look of concern on his face deepening before he realized that he too should sit.

"I know why you're here Penelope. As I stated before, I didn't see anything that night."

Rather than instantly refute his claim, Penelope decided to learn more about why he was so adamant about not seeing anything.

"If you're worried about a scandal, Walter, think of the bigger scandal that will ensue once the body is discovered and someone comes looking for suspects. You remaining silent despite having seen something wouldn't look very good."

Walter swallowed and nervously pushed his glasses up on his nose and gave her a pained look. "Why should I be involved at all? I wasn't a witness to anything," he said almost pleadingly. He turned to Detective Prescott. "Has a case officially been opened, detective?"

Penelope's brow rose in surprise. "How did you know he's a detective?"

"It's my job to read people. He has the look about him. You *are* a detective aren't you?"

"I am, and no there hasn't been a case officially opened...yet," Detective Prescott answered.

"Well, then, I'm not exactly sure how I can help you," Walter said almost defiantly.

"I know for a fact you saw the body that night, Walter. You admitted as much."

"How is that?"

"When we came down from the top and met you and Mona in that small room, I stated that I'd seen a body."

"Yes, I remember that."

"Do you remember what you said in response?"

He stared at her, his brow still furrowed in confusion.

"'Are you sure she was dead, Pony?' Those were your exact words."

"I still don't see how..." His brow smoothed when he realized his mistake.

"I didn't say whether it was a female or male. You already knew because you'd seen her through the windows of that small room."

The color drained from his face. "Yes, b-but...even if I had...my glasses were completely covered in rainwater. And I certainly didn't see any murder take place!"

"Walter..."

"I can't be involved in this, Pen. It was bad enough getting arrested, Mona's been in a state and Ducky is already in trouble with his parents."

"Have they contacted you about this?" Penelope asked in surprise. It now occurred to her why Mona was so sure Walter would agree with them that there was no body.

"What?" he asked, a guilty look instantly coming to his face. "I don't know what you're talking about."

"Oh stop Walter, you were never able to tell a good lie. What is it that you really saw that night? Forget about what Ducky or Mona asked you to say. After all, there is a detective here."

"I...I only denied it out of concern. Mona just seemed so distraught. And of course Ducky too," he added quickly.

Something suddenly occurred to Penelope. "Oh Walter, please don't tell me you're sweet on Mona."

His face went bright red in response. No, he was never one to be able to maintain a good lie.

"Mr. Adams, as you surmised I am in fact a detective. If you have any information related to this it's in your best interest to tell us right now," Detective Prescott said in a tone that didn't allow for sympathy.

"I...may have...also seen someone running away from the fountain."

"What?" Penelope exclaimed. "And this whole time you never said a word about it?"

"It was just a person running. They weren't even headed to the Whitley residence, so it couldn't have been one of them like you suggested. It was so dark, and my glasses were so wet, I couldn't even tell you if it was a man or a woman. There were a lot of scamps in the park that night. I just assumed it was one of them."

"Which direction were they headed?" Detective Prescott pressed.

"Down one of the pathways southward, into the trees, toward the more unsavory side of the park."

"I assume they weren't carrying the body?" Pen asked, mostly sarcastically.

"No," Walter replied in a droll voice.

"Still," Penelope interjected, "they could have been the person who killed her and left her body there in the first place."

"But why would they be heading south in the opposite direction of the Whitley residence?"

She thought of Ducky shouting from the top of the arch: "I see you!"

"Maybe it was so they could avoid bringing suspicion upon themselves. Or maybe they were scouting a place to move the body later on, which they obviously did."

"Or it was just a scamp trying to escape the rain," Walter countered.

"Can you describe anything about this person at all?" Detective Prescott asked.

"As I said, I couldn't even tell you if it was a man or a woman. They were wearing a coat and a hat."

"Was it a man's hat or a woman's hat?" Penelope pressed.

Walter shifted in his seat. "I suppose it was a man's hat and trench coat. But that's all I can tell you! I don't know if he was tall or short. I don't know what color his hair was. I couldn't even tell you what race he was. Just a man...or it could have been a woman in a man's clothing. You know what those bohemian artist types are like down there."

"Why did Mona or Ducky tell you not to say anything?"

"They just don't want a scandal. Is that so hard to understand? We can't all inherit five million dollars, Pen. Some of us have to work and maintain a good reputation for our parents' sake. I can sympathize with Ducky. His parents have cut him off, forcing him to get a job and everything. Why should Mona have to suffer the consequences of some mystery woman traipsing through the park at night and getting murdered?"

"Unless she was murdered by one of the Whitleys."

"Well, that's hardly likely based on what I saw, is it? I wasn't lying about what direction I saw this person run."

That was something Penelope had trouble understanding. Why head south instead of directly north back to their home? The only thing she could think was that they *were* trying to avoid suspicion by going in the opposite direction, or just hiding in the nearest trees.

There was also still the more puzzling question of why they came back to remove the body later on?

"That's all I know, I swear, Penelope. At the time, I didn't think the information was relevant, and it seemed like it would cause more problems than it solved. You still don't have a body, even now," Walter accused. "Now if you don't mind, as I said, some of us have to work for a living," he said with a note of finality.

"Thank you for your time, Mr. Adams," Detective Prescott said, rising from his chair.

Penelope didn't want to leave so soon. She was angry with Walter for hiding information. All this time she had looked like a hysterical woman making up tales, and he had seen something that might support her claims.

She rose and joined Detective Prescott to leave. Once back outside, she felt more emboldened. "Now do you believe me about the murder?"

"I never doubted you, Penelope," Detective Prescott said in a sincere tone. "But it's still rather difficult to open a case without a body. Even with this information that doesn't give us much."

"We can be certain it was a man, can't we?"

"Or, as he said, a woman dressed as a man. He's right, in these times it's not such an outrageous idea."

"Especially in that part of New York," Penelope conceded. It had been a recent fad for women to dress up as men, at least so openly. She herself could attest to the fact that there was a certain freedom and exhilaration that came from wearing pants the few times she'd dared to try it. "I suppose we'll have to wait until tonight's party to glean more. Maybe Andrew will give us the missing piece of this ridiculous puzzle. You are still coming tonight, aren't you?"

"It is my job, ma'am."

"I think it best if we arrive separately. At least a few

people know you're a detective, and I'd rather not have that hindering my progress."

"Hindering? I hadn't realized I was such a burden," He said with a grin.

"Never. But I'm still having trouble seeing you as anything but a detective. Walter was right, you are quite obvious about it."

"Then prepare to be surprised, Miss Banks."

Penelope studied him with a growing smile. "Well, well, well, I have a feeling tonight is going to expose quite a bit. I for one look forward to it."

CHAPTER TWENTY-FOUR

PENELOPE DECIDED TO GIVE LEONARD THE NIGHT OFF. Knowing that Detective Prescott would be at the party as well, she could at least be assured of an escort home. The area east of the park was still somewhat lively at this hour of the night. As such, when she arrived at the building a block away from the park, there were already ossified revelers approaching the front door at the same time.

It was a trio, two women and a man. The woman draped over the man's arm was wrapped in a huge embroidered shawl with fringe that covered whatever she was wearing underneath.

The other woman—who had a pitch-black, Dutch cut hairstyle that was rarely flattering, but looked positively divine on her—gave Penelope a considering look as she smoked a cigarette in a long, gold holder. She was wearing a black, silk pajama set—flared pants and a buttoned, long-sleeved top—covered in a gold koi fish pattern.

Penelope had worn her shortest black dress overlaid with gold lace, and she couldn't tell if she felt overdressed or underdressed. Perhaps just inappropriately dressed. She probably would have fit in better if she had worn the Japanese kimono she had stolen from a hotel recently. One day she would have to come back to one of these parties wearing just that, if only to soothe her pride that she wasn't completely out of fashion.

"Are you here for the Gadot party?" the one in the pajamas asked in a husky voice, a subtle smirk touching the corners of her mouth.

"Yes, I was invited by Andrew Whitley?" She reminded herself that she was here to solve a case, not to win acceptance from the artists of Greenwich Village.

"Andrew?" The man asked, a grin coming to his face. "Is that old fool coming? Well, ladies, we can be assured of some decent hooch tonight, along with other vices," he added waggling his eyebrows.

"We ain't gonna commit any vice standing out here on the street," the woman on his arm said with a pout.

The woman in the pajamas turned the handle of the door, and Penelope was surprised when it opened for them. She certainly hadn't expected a doorman to be manning the front door, but it seemed these buildings really were open for the taking. She wondered how long that would last.

She followed the three inside. The first level was one big open floor, dark and covered in dust and debris. It had obviously once been a warehouse or factory. They walked to a set of stairs at the back that took them up to the second floor. This level had former offices lining the walls, but the party was in the main open area in the middle. The only lighting came from candles situated on almost every surface, being that the building probably wasn't electrified. Penelope thought back to the horrible shirtwaist factory fire that had happened only a few blocks from here when she was ten. At least this was only on the second floor should everyone need to escape.

The man and woman skipped off to greet some fellow partiers, leaving the third woman with Penelope.

"I haven't seen you at one of these shindigs before."

"No, this is a first for me," Penelope said drinking in her surroundings. A woman stood on a small table further away doing some sort of eastern dance, snaking her hips and arms. She wore harem pants and a cropped top that showed not only her entire torso down to the navel but at least a few inches below that. This was all rather thrilling.

"I'm Sonia by the way, Sonia Paraffin," the woman said, drawing Pen's attention back. She held out a hand for Penelope to shake.

"Penelope Banks, but you can call me Pen." She studied Sonia. "So you're an artist?"

"Tragically," the woman said with a laugh. "I suppose that much is obvious, huh? I'm the painting sort, not the theater sort like your boy Andrew adores. And you?"

"Just another boring wealthy socialite."

That earned her a hearty laugh. "I doubt there's anything boring about you. I have a nose for these things. Come, let me show you around."

She hooked her arm through Penelope's and they strolled around. She grinned when Pen's eyes landed on a table covered in...candy?

"That's Brenda's doing," Sonia said, following her gaze. "Her father owns the Marcell Candy stores you see all over town? She gets her jollies stealing as much as she can from him," Sonia said, releasing Penelope's arm to boldly dip her hand into the bowl of jelly beans and scoop some up. Penelope satisfied herself with a butterscotch candy stick.

Sonia showed her around introducing her to dancers

and artists and models and those who orbited their worlds. This was exactly how she imagined these sorts of parties to be, filled with interesting characters. It reminded her of the dinners her mother used to host with a motley mix of fascinating personalities. One of these days she'd have to host her own dinner. Perhaps Sonia could be one of her first guests.

At the very least she wouldn't have to worry about Detective Prescott standing out too much. Even with his scar, it was unlikely that either Ruth or Andrew, if they were in attendance, would notice him as soon as he stepped foot in the door, the place was so crowded.

There was a huge crystal punch bowl that must have cost a fortune filled with a bright pink concoction. It never ceased to amaze Penelope the mix of high and low that could be found in New York City. She poured herself some into a chipped teacup and cautiously sipped. It was far too sweet and she didn't immediately taste any alcohol. She knew from experience, those were usually the most dangerously potent types of drinks. Sonia grabbed a wine glass and ladled a generous amount into it for herself.

"If you're looking for Andrew, just look for the gals with the most comely gams. That is his favorite bit of anatomy," she said with a grin.

"Do you know him well?"

"Well enough to know he's hoping to become the next Ziegfeld."

"So what's stopping him?"

"The same things that stopping us all, sweetheart. But lately, he's been bragging about how that little obstacle will soon be overcome."

"Is that so?" So Ruth wasn't the only Whitley sibling

expecting to land in a pile of kale. "Do you think he'll be successful?"

Sonia laughed. "Oh Pen darling, I know a good time boy when I see one. Andrew likes to play at being the poobah. He should stick to wooing flappers and leave the business to the big boys."

"So you don't think he'll be a success."

"I don't think even he thinks that. Some men are all bark and no bite." She chomped her teeth together, which made Penelope laugh. "At any rate, Pen darling, it was nice meeting you but I must socialize. Though, I have a feeling you and I might run into one another again," she said mysteriously before disappearing into the crowd.

Penelope was left to people watch on her own. That was certainly enough to entertain her for the moment. The party was filled with a certain type, mostly young, mostly frivolous, mostly poor, or playing at it. It nearly made her nostalgic for the days she was in the same position, when her hedonistic nights were spent mostly in jazz clubs and illegal gambling backrooms.

Her eyes were instantly drawn to the top of the stairway where Detective Prescott was arriving. Even without the hat and the suit, the man drew the eye. It wasn't just the scar on the side of his face, it was that he was so damn handsome. Penelope had never seen him in casual clothes. He wore a fitted lightweight jacket that outlined a broad chest and the muscles of his shoulders and arms. His dark hair was combed back to make him appear more youthful. All it did was show off his handsome face. When a zozzled young flapper literally threw herself at him, Penelope wanted to rush over and snatch her away. He handled it well enough, grinning down at her and easily detaching her arms from his shoulder, then handing her back to her friends.

Penelope looked away and was surprised to find her eyes landing on Andrew. That was certainly enough of a distraction to make her forget about her detective. Mostly because Andrew was in the middle of a heated conversation with David Cranberry.

Penelope stepped behind a group of people to hide as she observed them. If David was telling Andrew about his run-in with Detective Prescott and her, that would ruin everything.

She moved in closer while staying hidden behind a group of girls who were lamenting over the scoundrel one of them was involved with. Pen strained her ears to listen in on the men's conversation and only managed to hear half of it.

"... hadn't shown up on our doorstep like some love-struck fool and...never would have...that we actually knew the damn woman! Frankly...my money back!"

"Oh no you don't....asking for more money!... think I killed her."

"...you idiot! That's the story we're going with....no body, and no one has...far as the police know, she was—"

"Hey wait a second that's the woman! Banks something."

Penelope realized she had been found out by David, who was pointing right at her. There was no more use trying to disguise herself. She extricated herself from the group of girls and boldly approached the two men.

"Yes, it's me," she said addressing David. She turned her attention to Andrew. "At this point, there's no use claiming you have no idea who that woman in the park was. Why did you hire David here to run into her on the train? Did you know she wasn't really your cousin at the time?"

"I don't have to answer any of your questions," Andrew snapped. "Whatever it is you think you heard just now, the point remains, there is no body. My real cousin is safely asleep at our home right now, feel free to check if you want to wake her up at this late hour. I'm sure William will be thrilled."

He twisted around and walked away leaving Penelope staring after him. She turned her attention to David.

"Oh no you don't," he protested. "I told you all I know. Just leave me out of it, lady."

He too walked away leaving Penelope floundering on her own.

Unfortunately, that's also the moment she saw three of the law students enter the party, Georgie, Cal, and Thomas. Of course, Ruth was with them. The last thing she wanted to do was get embroiled in a discussion with any of them, especially as Georgie already appeared half liquidated. He garrulously shouted and grabbed the nearest woman to hug into his side in an impromptu dance, causing her to laugh with delight. Penelope slinked off into a corner, hoping she'd run into Detective Prescott, wherever he might be. She spent the time finishing off her butterscotch stick and observing the other partiers.

"Caught you," she heard a voice say right behind her, causing her to start in surprise.

She spun around to confront Detective Prescott. "You startled me."

"I didn't mean to. I thought I'd lost you for a moment. I got caught up in a discussion with Ruth Whitley, who spotted me right away, unfortunately. She seems awfully amused by the murder of this mysterious woman. Her cohorts not so much."

"They're former law students. They're probably tired of hearing about it by now." Penelope caught sight of Ruth in a heated discussion with Thomas. She had probably been teasing him again. One of these days, his jealousy would come to a head. Penelope turned her attention back to Detective Prescott. "Did you learn anything else?"

"Only that I would be more than welcome if I ever decided to pose for an artist. I have a feeling it wasn't putting charcoal to paper that she had in mind."

Despite their reasons for being there, Penelope laughed. "Are you trying to make me jealous?"

"Are you?"

"I must confess, you do dress down quite well. I'm inclined to ask you to pose for me as well, though I'm not an artist."

He laughed.

"I suppose I'll settle for that dinner you promised. That is if all your affairs are in order?"

Before he could respond there was a scream, loud enough to rise above the music, laughter, and chatter.

"Oh my God, he's dead!"

CHAPTER TWENTY-FIVE

"MAKE WAY," DETECTIVE PRESCOTT DEMANDED AS HE plowed ahead of Penelope through the crowd. "I'm an officer of the law. Please step back!"

They followed the sound of the woman's screams, which had subsided into sobs. They reached a group of people huddled over the body, staring down at it with morbid fascination.

"Stand back, now!" Detective Prescott ordered, his rich, strong voice capturing everyone's attention. They immediately took two steps back. Penelope came in around him and saw that the body on the floor was that of David Cranberry, who looked like he had been stabbed in the chest. She whipped her head back up and scanned the crowd.

Detective Prescott did the same. "I need everyone to remain here. No one is allowed to leave. Is that understood?"

There was a mumble of agreement, most of it disgruntled.

"Perfect, now settle down everyone," Detective Prescott

said. "First, I need Andrew Whitley and Ruth Whitley to please step forward."

There was some shuffling in the crowd and after half a minute Andrew slowly stepped forward looking perfectly stricken. He stared down at David's body in horror. Then, his eyes rose to meet the detective, filled with alarm. He knew he was the main suspect.

They waited a few moments until it became obvious that Ruth wasn't going to make an appearance.

"Where is Ruth Whitley?" Detective Prescott demanded looking angrily at the crowd. "Has anyone seen her?"

It was Calvin who spoke up. "I think she and Thomas left a moment ago, just before this business."

Penelope met Detective Prescott's gaze. That certainly wasn't the action of an innocent party.

"Did anyone see anything?" Detective Prescott asked looking around. He was met with nothing but shrugs and frowns, a few women were discreetly whimpering. He sighed in resignation. "Fine then, as I said no one is allowed to leave the room for now until the police arrive."

He turned to Penelope. "I need you to find a phone and call the police and tell them what happened. Let them know we need several officers for crowd control."

"There's no electricity in the building."

"I live nearby." Penelope recognized the scratchy purr of Sonia's voice. She made her way to the front of the crowd. "You can use the phone at my place."

Detective Prescott eyed her. "Alright, but you're to return here for questioning after that."

"Yes, detective," Sonia said with a wry smile.

She led Penelope down to the first floor and outside.

"Downer of a way to end a party, isn't it?"

"Particularly for David Cranberry."

"Yeah, poor Davey."

"Did you know him?"

"Oh, yes, but I'm probably one of the few gals there who didn't know him in the way he would have liked."

"Is that to mean that most of them knew him in *that* way?"

"Most of them were smart enough to end it at simple flirtation. He's a handsome fella yes, but two starving actors or artists in a relationship ain't no kind of fun. Your boy Andrew, on the other hand? Quite the target for many a quivering heart, especially the broke ones."

So, Dave was a cake eater. That certainly broadened the scope of suspects. Still, Penelope wasn't willing to dismiss the coincidence at hand. He had a direct connection to Mary Tate, and now he too had been murdered in almost the same way. There were at least two people with connections to both people in attendance tonight, Ruth and Andrew.

They turned a corner and crossed the street to a nearby apartment building. It was fairly modern, and the foyer was well-lit and decorated in a lively Art Deco design. Either Sonia's art was quite popular or she was being handsomely subsidized.

The one-room apartment she led Pen to was small and cozy but artfully decorated. The walls were covered in paintings and drawings that traversed the scope of styles and mediums. Against one wall was a mattress on the floor covered in colorful sheets and too many pillows. An overstuffed armchair draped with gorgeous outfits in fine fabrics was pushed against one corner. There was a large antique oak table that seemed to be a combination desk, dining table, and bookshelf.

An easel with a half-finished painting stood in a corner. It was the figure of a man, so abstract that Penelope couldn't even tell if he was clothed or not. Considering the artist, she would have put her money on the latter.

"Welcome to the typical artist abode. I get paid in favors of the artistic kind. Who knows, maybe by the time I'm ancient, one of these will be the next Mona Lisa and worth something?" She waved her hand around the room at the various works hung. "At any rate, here's the phone."

Penelope took hold of the receiver and asked to be connected to the police, repeating everything Detective Prescott had told her, then hung up.

"So, you and that detective, are you an item?" Sonia asked as they left the apartment to head back.

"Potentially," Penelope said, arching an eyebrow her way.

Sonia laughed. "Oh don't worry honey, Wasn't going there. I just think it's interesting he trusts you with so much."

"Well, I'm also a private investigator in my own right."

"You don't say? Why that's swell!"

Penelope felt a proud smile come to her face. She dug into her purse and handed Sonia a card. "If you ever need my services. I'm particularly affordable to help those in most need."

"Well, well," Sonia said, eyeing the card. "Ain't that something."

Back at the scene of the crime, the atmosphere was now more subdued. People had instinctively sectioned themselves off into smaller groupings, whispering among themselves as they cast furtive glances Detective Prescott's way. Penelope knew how quickly a calm crowd could turn into a mob that could easily overwhelm a single detective, no matter how strong he was.

Fortunately, the sound of sirens quickly followed her arrival. The police stormed in and worked with Detective Prescott to maintain control. Now that the shock of seeing a dead body had worn off, the crowd was getting restless and disgruntled.

Realizing he had no reason to keep everyone in attendance, Detective Prescott instructed the officers to get names and addresses. He also instructed them to do a thorough check of their person and belongings to make sure that they didn't have any evidence of blood or a weapon on them. Then they were free to go.

In the meantime, he and Penelope took Andrew outside to question him in private, since he was indeed the main suspect.

"It wasn't me, I swear!" Andrew cried before either of them could ask a question.

"But you do admit to knowing David Cranberry?" Penelope asked.

"Of course, but you already know that. That doesn't mean I killed him."

"Who else at the party might have known him enough to want him dead?" Detective Prescott asked.

Andrew looked completely and utterly hopeless. "I don't know. At least half the people here are actors or actresses like he was. So of course they know him. Maybe his murder had nothing to do with—"

He stopped himself before he could admit that there was a connection between David and himself.

"Now is the point at which you're going to tell us everything," Detective Prescott said. "And before you think of lying, Miss Banks and I already had a discussion with Mr.

Cranberry earlier. He told us quite a bit, so we'll know if you're holding back."

Penelope could see Andrew thinking about doing just that for one brief flash of a moment before he numbly nodded. "Okay."

He reached into a pocket and pulled out a pack of cigarettes. After placing one into his mouth with a trembling hand, he patted his other pocket as though in search of a lighter.

"Damn," he whispered, as though he just now remembered he didn't have one. "Either of you got a light?"

Both Penelope and Detective Prescott shook their heads no.

"Damn," Andrew whispered again, removing the cigarette.

"Now start from the very beginning," Detective Prescott said in a slightly gentler voice.

Andrew sighed and stuffed the cigarette back into the pack, then shoved it into his pocket. "I know David from the theater. I like to spend time with a lot of the actresses and dancers," he said almost sheepishly. "When father got sick, we all knew he sent a letter out to our cousin, Susan. When Mr. Willis asked her to come to New York, we figured it had something to do with the will. Father always made it clear that everything he had wasn't *necessarily* ours for the taking upon his death. He liked to lord it over us," he said bitterly.

"When William told me Susan was coming out. I thought I could learn something about father's plans directly from her, but I couldn't very well meet her myself, could I? Everyone would notice if I disappeared for a few days only for them to discover that I had met up with her beforehand. So I hired David. He was good at playing the *Lothario*, and I knew he needed the money. I lent him an old suit of mine to look the part. Even then, he insisted I take him to Delmonico's, the ungrateful bastard." Andrew seemed to realize what he had just said and his eyes flashed in a panic. "That doesn't mean I killed him though."

"Just continue with your story," Detective Prescott urged.

"Well, everything seemed to go according to plan. He even had this whole scenario set up where he'd play the rescuing knight, just to seal the deal with her. I thought it was all rather genius, at least until he got back to New York. He told me he had the woman wrapped around his finger, but he wouldn't give me any information unless..." he paused, swallowing hard as though he knew he was about to reveal incriminating information. "...unless I paid him more money. I realized my mistake in hiring the scoundrel too late. He'd always been a charlatan."

"Tell us about Mary Tate, the woman who arrived before the real Susan Bennett who's now at your house."

"That's as much a mystery to me as it is to you! According to William, *she* was the real Susan Bennett. When she showed up we all assumed as much. I should have known better, the way William kept her from speaking too long with any of us. He was the one who set that whole thing up, wasn't he?"

Neither of them confirmed as much, but the look on Andrew's face seemed to already know the truth of it all. "Anyway, the next morning she was gone, and good riddance. Pretty sure the little tart stole one or two things on her way out."

"You didn't see her leave yourself?" Detective Prescott asked.

"No, I was asleep."

"Did you hear any arguments or shouting that night?"

"As I *said*, I was asleep. I couldn't have even told you there was a thunderstorm that night."

Penelope hoped that Detective Prescott wasn't *necessarily* believing his statement.

"And when did you learn about the second Susan Bennett? The *real* Susan Bennett?"

"William told us that morning before you arrived. He said you had come knocking in the middle of the night asking about that other woman. Said we weren't to tell you anything about her because, apparently, she had been a fraud who may very well have gotten herself killed. He told us any one of us could have the murder pinned on us. Considering what I'd done, hiring David and all, I thought it best to go along with that story."

"Did your brother or sisters know that you had hired David?"

"As far as I know, they didn't." He seemed to realize how that looked and suddenly he sagged against the wall. "Who says his death is even related to my hiring him? Any one of those people at the party could have killed Dave for any number of reasons. He was a bit of a rake, after all. Handsome, charming, he's broken more hearts than I can count. And most of his dalliances didn't exactly end on pleasant footing."

"But you were the only one that was seen arguing with him," Penelope accused.

"Why would I kill him! You already knew about him, so it isn't as though I had anything to hide."

"Maybe he discovered you were the murderer?"

"I *wasn't*! I was asleep that night. That woman, Mary or whatever, was very much alive when I went to sleep. The next morning I'd been told she had left, and that the real Susan Bennett was coming, which was a surprise to me."

"And you didn't think to ask any hard questions? Particularly after the two of us showed up that morning and mentioned that she might have been murdered in the night?"

"I already said I had my own reasons for staying quiet. I apologize for that. But is it a crime? Isn't there some constitutional amendment about not incriminating myself or something?"

"Can you think of any reason any of your siblings may have wanted the imposter Susan dead? Or perhaps even the real Susan?"

"No, I don't," he said firmly, giving Penelope a hard look. She almost admired his family loyalty. Certainly more than Ruth had.

One of the policemen approached them holding up a knife with a handkerchief. "Detective, it looks like we found our murder weapon. It had been tossed into a corner."

While everyone else was focused on the blood that covered the blade, Penelope was drawn to the handle. It was gold and inlaid with mother of pearl. The kind of knife that might be described as a handsome little devil, fit for a king.

The kind of knife that might even be an heirloom.

CHAPTER TWENTY-SIX

ANDREW HAD BEEN TAKEN AWAY BY ONE OF THE policemen to the station for further questioning, despite his protests that he was innocent. Penelope and Detective Prescott were still standing on the street outside.

"I think I know that knife. I'm pretty sure that it belongs to George, one of the law students from the Golden Swan. He claimed it had been stolen."

Detective Prescott nodded and led her back inside and up the stairs. "Is there a George here?" He turned to Penelope. "Do you have a last name?"

"No," she said scanning the crowd to see if either he or Calvin was still here, "but I know he's one of the law students."

"Oh, you mean Georgie MacMillan?" A young woman said. "I know him, he comes to all these parties. He's already been questioned."

Detective Prescott got the address from the police officer who was taking everyone's information. It was not too far from there.

He and Penelope walked a block until they reached an

apartment building that, like Sonia's was slightly nicer than others in this part of town. Perfect for the young man intent on "slumming" with the lower classes, without dirtying the ends of his tailcoat too much.

"Hmm, no call system or doorman on duty this time of night."

"A locked door is hardly a deterrent for me." Pen pulled out one of the bobby pins holding her headpiece in place.

"I think not," Detective Prescott said when he saw what she was about to do.

"Why not?"

"Because that would be breaking and entering. And we don't have a warrant."

"But you *are* after a murder suspect aren't you? What would you do under normal circumstances?"

"Wait for a warrant of arrest and then break the door down."

"In other words damage property. And here's me, a good citizen, finding a perfectly acceptable alternative."

"Without the warrant," he reminded her.

"But I'm a member of the public, I don't need a warrant."

"Any other member of the public caught breaking and entering would be arrested on the spot."

"Even without a warrant?"

"Certainly while I had her in my clutches," he said with a glimmer of amusement in his eyes.

Penelope exhaled with impatience. "Fine then, I suppose you'll just have to arrest me for disorderly conduct for what I'm about to do."

His brow wrinkled as he watched her back walk into the middle of the street, her head craned back to look up at the apartment building.

"Hello! Is anyone awake? This is the police!" More than a few lights came on as she continued shouting.

"Miss Banks," Detective Prescott scolded. "That's hardly—"

"Why don't you shut your yap, chickadee?" someone yelled out of their window.

"Come down and make me, why don't you?" Pen taunted back with a smirk.

"I have a good mind to do just that!"

"Well then, what are you waiting for? You chicken?"

"Why you little—"

"Sir," Detective Prescott interrupted, back-walking into the street so he could be seen. He held up his badge. "I need you to come down and open the door for us."

"What is this some kind of prank?"

"No, I assure you, sir, this is official police business."

"Is it a raid?"

"It will be if you don't come down and open the door."

There was more grumbling before he disappeared. A minute later the front door was opened by a disgruntled man in his pajamas. "What's the big idea? Is this how the police are operating these days? Some of us are trying to—"

"Thank you for your cooperation, sir," Detective Prescott interrupted walking in past him. Penelope offered him a highly amused grin as she followed the detective.

They walked up the one flight to get to George's apartment and knocked. When he finally opened the door, he looked out at them with a wary expression.

"You weren't asleep already, were you?" Pen asked.

"No, but I was planning on getting there."

"Sorry to disturb you so late," Detective Prescott said.

"You might want to apologize to the whole neighborhood while you're at it. What can I do for you? I already answered all the questions from the police officer."

"Miss Banks here informed me that you mentioned losing a knife recently?"

"Wasn't all that recent." A line deepened in his brow. " Why?"

"Can you describe this knife for us?"

George understandably paused. His eyes darted back and forth between Penelope and Detective Prescott.

"I don't think I will. In fact, I think I'm going to invoke my Fifth Amendment rights."

"We can easily get the information from one of your friends who may have seen it. If I have to go through that much trouble I'm going to be far more inclined to come back here and put you in handcuffs just for making my job more difficult."

"So you're going to strong arm me, is that it?"

"This knife may have been used to kill a man tonight, George," Penelope said, placing a quieting hand on Detective Prescott's arm. "If it really was stolen, you might be able to help us find out who did it."

George ran a hand across his face and groaned. "Fine. It has a gold, etched handle, inlaid with mother-of-pearl."

Detective Prescott and Pen looked at each other. That was their murder weapon.

George saw it on their faces. "It really was stolen, just in case you think I'm lying. And I'm hardly the only one of my friends who had things taken. Just ask them! We all suspect it was Barry Henderson. He was one of our friends, used to sit with us by the fountain. At least until he was caught with Alfie's missing gold pen, a present from his parents when he first started law school. Cal said he had also stolen a pair of his cufflinks and a gold money clip of Tom's as well."

Penelope remembered Alfie mentioning something about Barry, that he was no longer a part of their group. "So he was found with all these stolen items?"

"Apparently, and he was expelled for it, rightfully so. But I never got my knife back did I? He denied he had taken it, but he said the same thing about all the other stolen loot as well. You think you know someone...."

"But the knife was never found in his possession?" Detective Prescott said.

"No, but that doesn't mean he didn't take it!"

"You didn't happen to see this Barry Henderson at the party tonight did you?" Pen asked with a heavy dose of skepticism.

"No," he replied in a patronizing tone. "But let's think here. Everyone has seen me with that knife. Like they told you that night at the Golden Swan, I was always playing a version of darts with it. Why would I then use it to kill someone? And then *leave* it at the scene?"

"Because the police were searching everyone as they left the party," Pen offered.

"Well, it certainly didn't take them long to find it, did it? It obviously wasn't very well hidden."

Penelope considered that.

"I'd say someone was trying to frame me. Probably the very someone who killed this David Cranberry."

"Did you know him?" Penelope asked.

George shrugged. "I'd seen him at parties before. Enough to recognize him that morning when he went to Ruth's house. Otherwise, he was never really my focus of attention, if you get my meaning. But I didn't have a reason to kill him. Where's your motive?"

That little tickle did present a problem.

"All the same we can't entirely eliminate you until we

have your fingerprints. Would you be willing to provide them?" Detective Prescott asked.

"At a decent hour of the morning," he said harshly. "*And* with my attorney in tow. I know my rights, detective, and you have absolutely no probable cause to arrest me or even take me in." George became as serious as Penelope had ever seen him. He leaned in closer toward them. "The fact is, I haven't had the knife for weeks now. Several people can attest to the fact that I claimed it was stolen long before this murder even took place. I barely knew David Cranberry and had absolutely no reason to kill him. I dare you to take this before a judge or jury. It would be laughed out of court. Now, will there be anything else, detective?"

Detective Prescott was surprisingly placid as he responded. "No, and thank you for your time, Mr. MacMillan. Enjoy the rest of your evening, or should I say, morning."

George responded to that with a puff of air before retiring inside and shutting the door on them.

"Do you think he did it?" Pen asked once they were outside again.

"No, I don't. He doesn't seem that stupid. But this business about the thefts is interesting. We obviously need to question his friends, see if they actually had things taken as well. I'm sure Mr. Henderson will continue to deny he took the knife. It showing up as the murder weapon makes me think maybe he was innocent."

"There were two other former classmates there, Thomas and Calvin. And of course Ruth. I know for a fact Thomas and Calvin live in the same building. If Thomas left with Ruth, they might both be at the same place right now."

"Perfect for a little interrogation."

"You're not concerned about the hour? Waking upstanding citizens of New York?" She teased.

"This time around we have an actual body, and conveniently enough, a murder weapon. No, I have no qualms here. Who knows, we may even find out who killed Mary Tate as well."

"Wouldn't that be something?"

As Pen led Detective Prescott down Washington Square South to the west side of the park, she considered all three candidates. Alfie wasn't there tonight. Perhaps an artist party didn't interest him? Neither were Mona and Ducky, at least as far as Pen saw. Why had they decided not to come?

Those were questions that could be answered later.

The front door to the building where Thomas' and Calvin lived was locked. Fortunately, there was a call system so Penelope reached out and pressed every button. They were eventually rewarded with a young woman bounding down the stairs in a robe and heading towards the beveled-glass front door. She stopped and gave them a quizzical look as she approached, obviously expecting someone else. Detective Prescott flashed his badge and her eyes went wide, but she hurried to open the door.

"Is there a problem officer?"

"No ma'am, we're just here to question some of your neighbors."

"At this hour?"

"Thank you for your assistance, please return to your apartment."

She clutched her robe shut and rushed back upstairs.

The door opened to a small, utilitarian foyer with a row of mailboxes to one side. Penelope walked over to scan the names on the boxes and found there were three Thomases.

She wasn't exactly sure which one was hers—she kicked herself for not getting that info from George while they had him. However, she did see that there was only one Calvin with the last name of Clemont.

"Well, we could bother all three Thomases in the wee hours of the morning or we can check with the one Calvin Clemont? I'd suggest the latter."

"At the very least he should still be up, or at least not fully asleep yet."

Penelope nodded as they took the stairs up to the second floor. Detective Prescott knocked on his door, and after a moment it was opened by Calvin. His eyes widened when he saw who it was. "Sorry, I thought you might be Thomas."

"We've actually come to question him as well," Penelope said. "We were wondering if Ruth was still with him. Unfortunately, there seem to be three Toms or Thomases in this building. Do you know which one is your friend?"

He gave them a sleepy smile and pointed down at the other end of the hall. "Thomas Frasier, in that one at the end of the hall. If he's not in, he might be on the roof. I know he likes to go up there and read or smoke. Not much of a view in his place."

"While we have you, just a few questions if you don't mind," Detective Prescott said.

Cal's mouth turned down in consideration, then he shrugged. "I told the officer at the party everything I know. I didn't see what happened at the party."

"This is specifically about the weapon we found."

"Oh?"

"As it turns out, it may have belonged to your friend George, the one he claims was stolen."

"You don't say? You found it?"

"Do you remember exactly when he first claimed it was gone?"

Cal thought about it for a moment. "It was about a month ago, I'd say, around the time we were taking our final exams. In fact, a couple of us had things go missing. Barry Henderson, he was the one who had them as it turns out. But now you think Georgie's knife was found at the party? As the *murder* weapon?"

"Your cufflinks, did you ever recover them from Mr. Henderson?" Detective Prescott asked rather than answer his question.

Cal breathed out a cynical laugh. "No, Barry still has the audacity to claim that he never stole them. Only Alfie got his pen back."

"I see, so you have no doubt that it was Barry Henderson who took your items?"

"Well, he was expelled wasn't he?" Calvin said as though that answered the question.

"You didn't happen to see him at the party tonight did you?" Penelope asked.

Calvin's mouth hitched up into a thoughtful half-smile. "No, which I guess does beg the question, doesn't it? Who really stole the knife?"

"Did you happen to know the victim David Cranberry?"

"No, that party really isn't the sort of thing I usually go to. Even the Golden Swan, isn't really of interest, but Wednesday nights a lot of former classmates have been going while we study for the bar. Obviously, once I take it, that will come to an end. That artist set, though, that's Georgie's sort of scene, we only came as a lark. In retrospect, I wish I'd followed Alfie's lead and bowed out as well. My time would have been better spent studying."

"You didn't see Ducky or Mona there, did you?" Pen asked.

"No. Are they suspects?"

"No, but they were the ones to invite me."

"Ah, well," he sighed in a way that hinted he would prefer to get back to bed.

"I have no further questions," Penelope said, turning to Detective Prescott next to her.

"I think that'll be all for now, thank you for your cooperation."

They left Cal to his bed and went to knock on Thomas's door. There was no response. After knocking once again, they both listened at the door but heard nothing.

"I suppose we should check the roof as Cal suggested."

They went up three more flights of stairs. The door leading to the roof was at the very end of the hallway and required one more flight to reach it. Since it was self-locking once closed, Detective Prescott left it slightly ajar before they went in search of Thomas and hopefully Ruth.

It was a large roof with a shed and water tower. They made a trek once around the entire roof and found no one.

"He isn't in his apartment and not up here, so where is he?" Pen asked. "Still with Ruth do you think? Maybe they went to her home instead?"

"We'll check his apartment one more time, then I'm afraid the Whitleys are in for another early morning wake-up knock."

They headed back to the door...only to find it firmly closed.

"I thought you left it propped open."

"I did," Detective Prescott said, staring hard at the door.

"Well, there's a lock, and it's a clear night with a nearly full moon. I suppose I could put my skills to use, if you have no objections, of course," Penelope said, giving him a wry smile.

He gestured towards the lock. "By all means, be my guest."

Penelope laughed and bent down, pulling a bobby pin from her hair again as she did. Unfortunately, the lock was rather rusty. It took her a while to do this under normal circumstances but even after minutes of jiggling her bobby pin, she found that—

"Oh!"

"Oh?"

"It broke."

"What broke?" Detective Prescott asked, dread filling his voice.

By way of answer, Penelope held up what was left of her bobby pin. The remainder was stuck inside the lock.

CHAPTER TWENTY-SEVEN

PENELOPE AND DETECTIVE PRESCOTT BANGED ON THE door of the roof for five minutes with no answer.

"It's a heavy door and it's all the way at the end of the hall. Someone would have to actually be up this late."

Fortunately, there were only a few hours left in the night. Come morning they'd be able to shout down to a passerby and send someone to rescue them.

"At least it's not too cold," Penelope said giving up on attacking the door. "I suppose that's one benefit to summer. It could also be raining like it was the night I went up the arch."

"Yes, that would make things ten times worse."

"Oh, I don't know," Penelope said with a smile, "There's something to be said for an outdoor shower."

"Now is hardly the time for flirting, Miss Banks," Detective Prescott said, but she could hear the humor in his voice.

"Even when he has me trapped alone on the roof, he ignores my advances," she mused.

"I hate to take advantage of you when you're so vulnerable," he said. "Though vulnerable is hardly an adjective I would use in your case."

Penelope walked toward the edge of the roof. "If we're going to be stuck here, at least give me the courtesy of calling me Penelope or Pen. I think I'm going to scream bloody murder if I hear you call me Miss Banks one more time."

"That might at least get us rescued," Detective Prescott said walking over to join her against the short wall that surrounded the edge of the roof. "But it would also raise too many questions. So be it, Penelope."

The two of them looked down on Washington Square Park. On such a clear night, it didn't seem so sinister. Yes, she could see the suspicious nocturnal denizens that made the park home when the daytime visitors were gone. Somehow even they didn't look all that threatening, not when murderers could be found amongst even the most upstanding citizens of the city.

"It seems they fixed the light," Penelope noted. "Now you can see the entire fountain."

"It's a rather nice view. At some point, the rest of the city is going to take note. Buildings like this won't last long. They'll be replaced by luxury residences, probably much taller."

"But for now it's all ours," Penelope said trying to paint the situation in the best light possible. "The only thing missing is candlelight and dinner."

"We do have the moon," Detective Prescott said looking up. Penelope heard something rustle as he reached into his pocket. "And I just so happen to have absconded from the party with this."

He held up a Hershey's chocolate bar.

"You didn't!" Penelope nearly squealed. Until he

revealed the candy bar, she hadn't realized how hungry she was.

Detective Prescott laughed as he unwrapped it and broke it entirely in half. He handed one part to her.

"Oh, I could just kiss you!" As soon as she said it she realized what she had just uttered. At the same time, her fingers whispered across his as she took the piece of candy from him and they both froze. Penelope wondered if this would be yet another disappointment, one where he decided his morals, ethics, or unresolved affairs posed some obstacle to him finally—

Those thoughts disappeared as his hand released the portion of candy he'd handed to her and came up to her neck. When this hand had held hers yesterday, it seemed large, now it seemed positively enormous. The back of his long fingers lightly grazed the nape of her neck, but she felt an intense heat rise from the skin underneath them. His thumb came up to stroke her jawline, and suddenly she felt like fire.

"Penelope..."

"Richard," she barely managed to breathe out.

What was left of her breath was taken away as he leaned down and pressed his mouth against hers. She instinctively came in closer and, even with his part of the candy bar in his other hand, he brought his arm around her waist and pulled her in the rest of the way. All those times she had wondered what his lips would feel like against hers were nothing compared to this. He was an awfully good kisser, his tongue waiting an appropriate amount of time before slipping out to explore first the inner part of her lips, then deeper into her mouth. She met it with her own and a slow rhythmic dance ensued.

Pen wasn't sure how long the kiss lasted but she was

almost reluctant when he pulled away. Still holding her in his arm, and with the other hand against the side of her neck, he stared down at her with a grin.

"I apologize. I think dinner was supposed to come before that."

Penelope smiled up at him. "I believe it's dessert that you gave me. Since we're doing everything backwards the kiss *should* come before that."

He laughed and pulled away, but still kept his arm around her waist. They settled down on the ground, their backs against the wall. They ate the chocolate in silence each of them grinning around the rectangular pieces.

When they were done Penelope turned to him. "I take it you have your affairs in order then?"

The smile on his face faded. "I do."

"Do you mind telling me what they were or would that be too intrusive?"

He turned to her with one eyebrow arched. "When has that ever stopped you?"

"You don't have to tell me," Penelope quickly assured him.

He chuckled softly. "It's a fair question considering everything. I was...giving my brother my blessing on his marriage."

That wasn't at all what Pen had expected him to say, and all it did was raise more questions.

As if reading her mind, Detective Prescott echoed her thoughts. "I'm sure that raises quite a number of questions, number one being why would my brother, who's two years older than me, need my blessing?

Penelope remained silent, allowing him to answer in his own time. There was obviously much more to this story, and as curious as she was she didn't want to press him on something so personal.

"It's a long and winding story," Detective Prescott said staring thoughtfully up at the sky.

"And it looks to be a long and winding night ahead of us. You might as well regale me," she said with a hint of humor that she hoped would encourage him.

Any remaining amusement in his face and voice completely disappeared. "It isn't exactly a happy story."

Penelope was sitting on the side of him that didn't show the scar, but she knew what it looked like, every detail of it. It wasn't too far-fetched to think that this story of his had to do with that scar from the Great War.

"My best friend growing up was a boy named Franklin Kent, Franky. We lived a few houses down from each other in a small town in New Jersey. As kids, we were inseparable despite how different we were. He was..." Detective Prescott turned to Penelope with a smile, "the *mischievous* one you might say. There wasn't a prank or dare or challenge he wouldn't instantly take on. I was always the voice of reason, always the one talking him down off the ledge or reminding him of the consequences."

Penelope felt a smile come to her face. That sounded awfully familiar.

"When the Wright brothers decided to change the course of history, he became obsessed with flying. As soon as we were old enough, we both learned to fly planes. I did it mostly to keep up with him, but I found I enjoyed it. In fact, I took to it quite well, perhaps even better than he did. He was of course more daring with it. When the war started, I wasn't surprised when he volunteered to join. Any chance to fly planes in a dangerous situation. His parents had the good sense to force him to wait until he graduated from college at least."

Detective Prescott was staring ahead as though reliving this history of his. He paused for so long that Penelope wasn't sure he would continue. Still, she didn't press him. They really did have all night.

"I didn't relish the idea of joining with him when he still had his mind set on joining. I knew enough about war to know the realities of it. There was a period of time when I was obsessed with the Civil War. Granted, there were no planes in that war, but war is...war." He paused again before continuing. "It was his little sister who finally encouraged me to go. She and I were..."

In the light of the moon, Penelope could see the subtle smile that came to his lips. It looked nostalgic and sad, but she couldn't help the ripple of jealousy that ran through her veins.

"Sophie had always been the bothersome little sister who tried to join all our activities and adventures. It wasn't until she turned sixteen that I actually noticed her, or more importantly, noticed the way she had always noticed me. I was two years older than her, and when she turned eighteen, we were finally engaged to be married. I couldn't very well let her brother go off to war without me. So I went with him."

There was another long pause during which Penelope filled in a lot of blanks herself. "He didn't come back did he?"

It took a moment for him to answer, and he shook his head slowly. "It was dangerous enough flying those damn planes. A lot of boys didn't even make it out of training. Franky did of course. One might even call him a hero, some of the feats he accomplished. It's hard to talk someone back from the ledge when you're in two separate planes. I saw him go down right before me, knowing there was nothing I could do to save him."

Penelope sucked in a breath, imagining the pain he'd had to go through watching his best friend die in such a horrible way.

"I spared his family the details, focusing on the valor more than anything. That's war for you, valor and death. The other side of that coin is where you find the longer-lasting effects. When I didn't hear back from them I assumed they were still in grief. Maybe they were. Either way, by then the U.S. had officially joined and I found myself with another year of flying. I suppose I was one of the lucky ones, if you could call it that." His hand idly reached up to touch his scar, his fingertips lightly tracing the other side of his jaw. I was shot down but I had enough control to at least land safely. Still, there was a fire and my leg was trapped for too long, long enough to give me my own souvenir of the Great War—at least beyond the point-less medals stored somewhere.

"I don't know what I was expecting by the time I made it home. The letters I had received from my parents were vague on the issue of the Kent family. I was of course willing to release Sophie from the engagement...for any reason she decided." His jaw tightened and his fingers inadvertently came up to his scar again. "What I hadn't expected was that she and my older brother, Michael, had fallen in love during those years I was gone.

"I wish I could say I'd been the better man. Maybe it was the combination of everything all at once, losing my best friend, the betrayal, and yes, this damn scar. I ignored their pleas for my forgiveness if not my blessing. I left for

New York and never looked back. I joined the police force and...the rest is history."

"So, was I the one who inadvertently led you to forgive them?"

He turned to her with a small laugh. "Penelope, you can make a man do any number of things. In a way, yes, I suppose you did. I probably forgave them a long time ago, I just couldn't bring myself to go back there and actually say as much to their face. Even I can be petty sometimes, be forewarned. I was never close to Michael for a number of reasons, but Sophie..." He exhaled heavily. "Mostly I just hated the way everyone else seemed to have moved on with their life while I was gone. I didn't attend the wedding. I still hadn't even met my two-year-old nephew. I realized I was still holding on to that last bit of anger." He studied her with intense eyes. "And then you came along."

Penelope realized she had learned more about Richard tonight than she had in the many months that she'd known him. He had always been so closed off, but at least now she understood why. She was glad she'd been able to help open him up. Suddenly she found herself curious about his family. But he had revealed so much tonight, she didn't want to *completely* intrude on his personal life. Besides she had a feeling this was only the beginning of things.

"Well, as far as dinners go, Richard, I'd say this is one of the more interesting ones I've had. I should have chocolate for dinner more often."

He laughed, his body relaxing next to hers. "Oh no, this is just dessert, remember. I think I still owe you a real dinner."

"Is there anything you'd like to know about me?"

He studied her with a subtle, enigmatic smile. "I find it more fun to reveal the layers of you at a gradual pace. I have a feeling if I asked, you would tell me everything and that would ruin the mystique."

"Mystique? I hadn't realized I was *that* interesting."

"Penelope, now is certainly not the time to start being coy," he said with a laugh.

"So will you call me Penelope on a permanent basis from now on?"

"Outside of official investigations, I suppose it's appropriate."

"Well, that hardly helps. Most of the time we interact it's during official investigations."

"Then I suppose I have to do something to rectify that, Penelope," he said with a smile.

Penelope pursed her lips. "I *should* make you work for it if you're going to be this difficult about things."

He laughed and brought his arm around her shoulders to pull her in closer. "For now let's just rest. I have a feeling tomorrow is going to be a day of revelations. Much more than tonight has been," he said softly.

Penelope felt the exhaustion of the evening set in. She supposed it wouldn't be a bad thing to get a few hours' sleep while they were stuck up there on the roof. She too had a feeling tomorrow might just be the day they solved this case.

CHAPTER TWENTY-EIGHT

"What the hell is this? I warned you kids about coming up to the roof like this!"

Penelope's eyes snapped open at the sound of that outraged voice. It took a moment to register where she was and why. She was outside, lying down with her head on a lap and a jacket draped over her upper body. She blinked in surprise when she remembered that both the lap and the jacket belonged to Detective Prescott—Richard. She would have to get used to calling him that now.

The way the man by the door was looking at her had her instantly sitting up and handing the jacket back to Richard.

"This ain't that kind of building, yous two. Whatever it is you wanna get up to, do it in the privacy of your apartment not out in the open like a couple of bohemian perverts. It was bad enough, all that water getting in from leaving the door propped open the other night. This is how rodents and bugs get in the building. Maybe being stuck up here overnight will finally teach you—wait a second! Yous two ain't residents of the building!"

Detective Prescott was the first to get to his feet. He took a moment to reach down a hand to help Penelope up before addressing the man. One flash of his badge had the man's expression softening. He was still wary, but at least he didn't look at them like they were two youngsters caught canoodling behind their parents' back.

"I'm Detective Prescott. We were trapped on the roof while investigating a murder."

"A *murder?*"

"We're looking for one of your residents, a Thomas Frasier?"

"Yeah? What's he done?" He squinted with suspicion.

"That's a police matter. Thank you for your assistance." Richard held on to Penelope's hand as he walked past the man holding the door open.

"Hey, wait a second, what happened to this lock!" they heard the man protest as they quickly descended the stairs. Penelope bit back a smile as they hurried down to Thomas's apartment.

"Don't worry, I'll pay for a new lock," Penelope said, knowing that Richard probably didn't find it quite as amusing.

"I'm more concerned about how we ended up stuck on the roof all night. I don't think that door closing on us was a coincidence."

"You think someone did it deliberately?"

"I know I was careful to leave it securely ajar. Yes, I think it was deliberate."

"Ruth and Thomas?"

"Let's find out, shall we?" He pounded his fist against Thomas's door in three loud knocks.

When he finally answered, Thomas didn't look particularly pleased about being woken so early in the morning.

"What are you doing here?"

"Making inquiries into the murder of David Cranberry."

"David who?" he asked looking genuinely confused, either that or putting on a good show. Then again, if he was the murderer he'd been putting on a pretty good show all week.

"He was at the party last night. The same party that you and Ruth attended, and then conveniently left right around the time of the murder—together, I believe?"

That was enough to have him fully alert. "Wait a second, you don't think Ruth or I had anything to do with that? Yeah, we left the party only because she didn't—"

He stopped as though catching himself before revealing something.

"Because she didn't what?" Penelope pressed.

His mouth hardened in resentment before he answered. "She didn't want her brother to see her there."

"Did she see the man with whom her brother was arguing?"

"I don't know. She was upset with Cal about something, as usual," he said rolling his eyes. "So I offered to leave with her."

"And is she still here with you?" Richard asked.

Thomas tilted his chin up in defiance. "That's none of your business."

"Need I remind you this is a police investigation into a *murder*?"

"Yes, yes, I'm still here," Penelope heard Ruth's voice call out. A moment later she slipped past Thomas to lean against the doorframe with an insolent smirk on her lips. "Who is it that got murdered again?"

"His name is David Cranberry, a friend of your brother's. You may have seen him arguing with him last night? He also came to your house the same morning Miss Banks and I met with your family."

She shrugged. "Doesn't sound familiar. Just why is it that I may have killed this David Cranberry?"

"That's a good question," Penelope said giving her an even look.

"We aren't *accusing* anyone of anything, just asking questions," Detective Prescott was quick to say.

"Neither of us has anything to hide," Ruth said.

"Then you won't mind if we search your apartment?" Richard asked.

"I certainly *do* mind," Thomas protested. "Don't you need a warrant or something for that?"

"Not if you give your permission."

"Well, you don't have it."

"Nonsense, Tommy," Ruth said with a sharp laugh. "If it ends all this nonsense, just let him search your apartment. We didn't kill anyone last night. At least you aren't the slob your friends are. You have nothing to be embarrassed about."

"I'm not worried about how clean it is. What if they plant something?"

"You're free to remain in the apartment and watch my every move," Detective Prescott assured him.

Ruth stared hard at Thomas. "Neither you nor I have anything to hide or worry about. This at least takes the blame away from us." She turned to look at Penelope with narrowed eyes. "Since this one is so set on blaming me for everyone who gets killed." She turned back to look at Thomas, giving him a penetrating look. "Let's just get it over with."

There was something she was conveying in her gaze,

something that finally had Thomas agreeing. He tore his eyes away from Ruth and glared at the detective and Penelope. "Fine, as she said, we have nothing to hide. Go ahead and search."

Detective Prescott stepped inside and Penelope followed, since no one seemed to object to it. Ruth was right, the apartment was cleaner than any single man's apartment had any right to be. She knew some people were rather obsessive about this sort of orderliness.

"Did you come straight here after you left the party?" Detective Prescott asked.

"We were smoking in the park for a while. I wasn't tired and I didn't feel like being confined in an apartment all night," Ruth said.

That must have been why they didn't answer the door last night.

Detective Prescott was being thorough, opening drawers and carefully going through perfectly folded clothes. Penelope was more than happy to leave him to it, instead focusing her attention on Thomas and Ruth. Having played cards to make ends meet for a number of years she considered herself a decent read of people. Ruth was imbued with her usual insouciance. Thomas looked uncomfortable, but she supposed anyone would if a detective was going through every inch of their apartment.

"How much do you know about what your brothers were up to regarding Susan Bennett?" Pen asked Ruth.

"What my brothers were up to?" She repeated with an overtly curious look.

"Certainly two Susan Bennetts showing up in the space of a few days had to raise your suspicions."

"William told us all about Mary Tate. He did it for father's sake, unnecessarily as it turned out."

"You believe his excuse?"

"Of course," she said, flapping her eyelashes innocently. Pen realized it didn't matter if she believed it or not, she certainly wasn't going to be forthcoming with them.

"And David Cranberry? You weren't aware of his involvement with anything?"

"I have no idea who David Cranberry is."

And there was the problem. Only Andrew seemed to have some connection to David. Still, murder seemed rather extreme just to keep David from telling his siblings about his little plan.

Then there was the knife. Penelope knew that was the key to everything. If they could find out who had originally taken it, she was certain they'd find their killer.

"I think...I've found a clue."

The sound of Detective Prescott's announcement had all of their eyes quickly snapping to him in surprise. He was walking from the open kitchen area, a thin gold bracelet hanging from one outstretched finger. There was a tiny gold music note dangling from the bottom of it.

"What is that?" Thomas asked, looking perfectly confused.

"She was wearing that," Ruth said, staring at him with wide accusatory eyes. "The fake Susan—Mary Tate, she had that on the day she came to our house. What are *you* doing with it?"

"I have no idea? Where the hell did you find it?"

"Hidden in one of your pots."

"You—you *planted* it!" he accused, pointing a finger at Detective Prescott as he backed away. "I knew it! You don't have a suspect, so you're planting evidence on me, the easiest target. This is a setup! I didn't kill anyone!"

"What did you do, Thomas?" Ruth asked.

"I didn't do anything," he yelled. His eyes narrowed with suspicion as he stared at her. "You! You planted that didn't you?"

"Me? Why would I do that?"

"Because you were worried about the suspicion being cast on you all before you could get all that money from your father," he spat. He stabbed his finger her way as he turned back to Detective Prescott. "She had every opportunity to plant that here. She is always in my apartment she could have hidden it at any time."

"Including the night of the thunderstorm?" Penelope asked, hoping he'd be too panicked to wisely remain silent.

"Of course, she was here that night! That's when she must have planted it."

"I didn't plant anything that night," Ruth said. "Why would I try to frame you?"

Thomas had just revealed something that was contradictory to an earlier statement he'd made back at the Golden Swan. He had bitterly suggested Ruth had been with either Calvin or George that night, and Ruth herself had claimed she had been with Calvin. So why would he admit she was here with him? More importantly, why wasn't Ruth correcting him?

"Oh stop it, Ruthie, everyone knows it's Cal you want. Maybe George. I was always your lackey, a pet dog sitting there waiting for scraps. The perfect chump to take the fall for you." He turned to Detective Prescott once again. "But she's the only one of us with a motive. I'm not dizzy enough for her to go to prison."

"You *know* I didn't kill anyone," Ruth said through gritted teeth.

"I don't know any such thing," He said with a bitter laugh.

"I have an alibi," Ruth said. "You don't."

"What? I just told them I was with you. Don't you start lying now, you little—"

"I mean before that. I was with Calvin right up until the point I came to your apartment. He'll be more than happy to tell them that. Do *you* have an alibi before that?"

Thomas looked stricken, the color draining from his face. "Oh no, no, no, no, you aren't pinning this on me. A *murder*?"

"All you had to do was keep your stupid mouth shut, you idiot. Now, look at you."

"Me? If you hadn't pressured me into letting him search —" Something seemed to dawn on him, and his eyes widened. "Why would I let them search my apartment if I knew I had such incriminating evidence here? In fact, *Ruth* is the one that really wanted you to search. Probably because she knew you'd find that bracelet."

All eyes turned to Ruth, who suddenly seemed to realize that Thomas had a point.

"Aha, the smoking gun!" Thomas said almost gleefully.

"I didn't kill anyone or plant anything!"

"Smoking," Penelope said, so softly she was surprised anyone could have heard it.

Richard, of course, was the one who did hear it. "What about smoking?"

"The cigarettes!" Penelope said louder, her eyes widening as she stared at Ruth. "You're the one who's been stealing things."

"What things?"

"George's knife, no doubt Calvin's cuff links and Thomas's money clip, and of course Alfie's pen. Barry Henderson used to sit at the fountain with all of you. Is that when you planted Alfred's pen on him?"

"You stole my money clip?" Thomas raged, which seemed almost absurd considering the much more pressing priorities of the moment.

"And, of course, the gold lighter Calvin had that day at the fountain," Penelope continued.

"What are you talking about?" Ruth asked.

"You borrowed a cigarette from him that day I first met you and your family. I watched you from the other side of Washington Square. You borrowed his gold lighter and never returned it."

"*His* lighter? *His* lighter?" Ruth laughed. "That lighter isn't his. It belongs to Andrew. If anything I was just recovering it for him."

"A likely story," Thomas spat. "So Ruthie is a thief after all, and most likely the one who—"

"Mr. Frasier, now would be the time where you should do yourself a favor and shut up," Detective Prescott said in a low, steady voice, his eyes still trained on Penelope who was now deep in thought. Blessedly, he took that advice.

Penelope continued to wrack her brain. So Calvin stole the lighter? Was he the thief then? Even if he was, that had no connection to the murders.

There was something definitely going on here, something that involved both Thomas and Ruth. The way Ruth had silently communicated something to Tom before allowing them to search. What was it?

"The rain!" Pen finally announced when it hit her.

"What about the rain?" Detective Prescott asked

"The apartment manager, the man who came to rescue us on the roof. He mentioned that rain had entered the building door that had been propped open earlier this week. There's only been one night of rain this week, the same night that Mary Tate was killed. One or both of you were up on the roof during that thunderstorm, the period when it rained hard enough for water to get inside the door you kept propped open. You would have seen her in the park during the storm. Maybe you even got a look at who killed her. Or...was it you who took the body away?"

Penelope saved her focus for Ruth. "So which one was it Ruth? Were you up there with Calvin or Thomas when you saw Mary in the park?"

"I was with Calvin before the rain started, he'll tell you as much." She turned to look at Thomas, who looked positively livid. "*He* must have been the one up on the roof and saw her. Maybe that's when he took the bracelet off her dead body. He probably let you search this apartment so he could accuse me of having planted it, all while looking innocent."

Thomas roared in anger and lunged for Ruth. Fortunately, Richard was quick enough to reach out and grab him, holding him back.

"How dare you—you vicious *Jezebel*! It was you and Calvin who killed her! Then you got me to go along, doing your dirty work for you after the fact."

"Shut up, you idiot!"

"Stop telling me to shut up!"

"What do you mean do her dirty work?" Penelope pressed, hoping Thomas's anger would have him revealing something yet again.

"Ruth came to my apartment, probably right after she and Calvin had killed that woman." He glared at Ruth. "That's why you wanted me to go to the roof in the middle of a thunderstorm, wasn't it? All that nonsense about it being romantic and exciting. And I was fool enough to go along with it. I actually have to give it to you, Ruth, you truly looked surprised when we saw her

240

body lying there by the fountain in that flash of lightning."

"*I'm* the fool? Who's the fool who came with me to move the body?" Ruth turned her attention to Detective Prescott, still holding Thomas back. "That's all we did, we took the body to an empty warehouse so no one would find it. That's certainly the only crime *I'm* guilty of. Before that, I was with Calvin, like I said. I have no idea what this one was up to!"

"You stupid girl, you just confessed to a crime! Do you realize what that means for me?"

"If you hadn't accused me, then I wouldn't have had to."

"Just...*don't* say another word, Ruth!"

Ruth decided to take his advice. Suddenly she and Thomas weren't so quick to accuse each other anymore. Penelope looked back and forth between the two of them. They were both like statues, no longer willing to reveal anything.

So these two had been the ones to move Mary's body. But, they hadn't killed her. Unless Thomas was right about Ruth and Calvin doing the killing, which didn't seem likely. So one of her other siblings had done the actual murder and Ruth, as Thomas had said, had done the dirty work of cleaning up after them.

"I think I can fill in the details. You probably panicked when you saw the body, Ruth. If your cousin— your *real* cousin—was dead, then your father would leave nothing to you or your siblings, that's what you told me at the Golden Swan, in front of several witnesses. However, if she was only missing, long enough for your father to die before she presumably did, then that would solve your problem. In this case, there *is* motive Ruth."

Detective Prescott continued where she left off. "More

so, if your cousin couldn't be located or was declared dead *after* your father died, of course, the rules of intestate would declare that all the money goes to *her* nearest relatives. That would be you and your siblings."

"That doesn't mean I killed her!" Ruth finally spat out. "This one is still on the hook for that! I was with Cal right up until I came here, you can check with him!"

"We'll be doing that shortly," Detective Prescott said. "The question remains, did you see who did the actual killing."

"No!" Both Ruth and Thomas answered at the same time.

Perhaps they were telling the truth. After all, according to Tallulah, William had kicked Mary out of the house before it began raining. If Ruth had urged Thomas to the roof once the storm started, that's when the body would have already been by the fountain. They wouldn't have had a better view of the mysterious person Walter had seen flee into the path covered by trees, so they may not know who the murderer was.

"As it stands, you two are under arrest," Detective Prescott announced. "I'll make the call to have you two taken to the station. Then, Miss Banks and I are going to have a nice little chat with Calvin Clemont to confirm Ruth's story."

CHAPTER TWENTY-NINE

BOTH RUTH AND THOMAS HAD BEEN CARTED AWAY TO the station, along with the bracelet found—or planted—in the apartment. Richard and Penelope walked down the hall to Calvin's apartment and knocked again.

This time he was quicker to answer, opening the door with curiosity written across his face. "I heard all the commotion, is it true Ruth and Thomas were arrested? Did they kill this fellow David something or the other?"

"David Cranberry," Penelope corrected.

"Ah yes, of course. Was there something else you needed from me?"

"We need to confirm the timeline for Ruth Whitley," Richard said. "She claims she was with you that night before she went to Thomas's apartment. Can you confirm this, and also confirm what times she arrived and left?"

"Of course," he said nodding. "Well, we spent that afternoon and evening together." He shot Detective Prescott a guilty smile. "I would say where we were, but I'd rather plead the Fifth. After that, yes she came here. Then, Ruth threw one of her infamous tantrums and I decided I'd rather spend the rest of the evening alone. She stormed off, I didn't know where, but apparently it was down to Thomas's apartment? Which is nothing unusual."

"When was this?"

"Oh, it was definitely late. Well, after midnight."

"Was it before or after it started raining?" Penelope asked.

Calvin studied her, his eyes slightly narrowed in thought before he answered. "I can't say exactly. I do know that when the worst of the storm hit she was well and gone."

"And you didn't see her or anyone else again after that?"

"No, why do I need an alibi?" he asked with a small laugh.

"I notice you have a window facing the park," Detective Prescott observed, looking past him into the apartment. "You didn't happen to see any of the activity out by the fountain that night, did you?"

Calvin laughed again.

"I fail to see what's so humorous about a woman being killed," Penelope scolded.

"Of course," Calvin said becoming suddenly serious. "I wasn't laughing at that, I was laughing at the idea that I can see much of anything of the park through my windows. In fact, why don't you come in and see for yourselves?"

Detective Prescott and Penelope didn't need a second invitation to enter.

"As you can see, I have a perfectly lovely view of...trees."

At the window, Penelope couldn't see anything below the tree line. This included not just the fountain and the lights, but even The Row beyond the arch, which itself was only just barely visible above the treetops.

"Was there anything else you needed?" Cal said behind them.

She spun around to face him."The lighter you were using that day in the park, where did you get it from?"

Calvin stared at her, blinking once, then twice. "What lighter?"

"The one I saw you with. The one Ruth took from you to light her own cigarette? It was gold, I'm sure *she* could describe it in more detail."

Pen could almost see the machinery in his head working to come up with the right answer. "Oh, that lighter! That's actually Ruth's, or one of her brothers' I think. She must have let me borrow it at some point. In fact, I think she took it back that day."

"When was it that she first lent it to you?"

"I have no idea. What does that have to do with anything?"

"It's funny, we were questioning Andrew earlier. He was looking for that lighter. I'm guessing it's his only one. It's too bad, he really could have used the cigarette as he was quite stressed."

"Well, hopefully, *Ruth* returns it to him; and then learns to stop taking things that don't belong to her," Calvin said.

Watching him become upset satisfied a theory Penelope was working with. She decided to go all in with it. During her years playing poker, she knew exactly when to call a bluff, and Calvin might as well have been showing her every card he had in his hand.

"It's funny though, he seemed to be under the impression that Mary Tate had taken it that night when she left the Whitley home."

If the name meant anything to him, he didn't show it.

"Mary was the woman that I saw murdered that night.

She'd been kicked out of the Whitley house earlier, just before the thunderstorm started. That was around the time that Ruth left your apartment?"

Calvin's eyes narrowed with suspicion. "How would I know anything about that? Being that my window doesn't exactly give me a view of what goes on in the park or the Whitleys' home. Maybe you should be asking *Ruth* this question."

"But we're asking you," Detective Prescott said taking over. "If Andrew's lighter was taken *that* night, how did you come into possession of it by the next morning?"

"As I said, Ruth gave it to me. In fact, it was that morning. Yes! That's when she lent it to me."

"When exactly that morning? Because you said she was with you all afternoon and evening the day before, and then she went to Thomas's apartment. Yes, at some point she went home, where she remained all morning. The only time she came out again was on her way to school where she finally joined you in the park. That's when she took the lighter back. But when did she give it to you in the first place? And before you think about lying, how sure are you that she'll support your story?"

Calvin stared at them for a long moment. "It's a lighter. It doesn't mean a damn thing. It certainly isn't *proof* of anything."

"It's proof that you were in the Whitley house at some point that night," Pen said. "You like to steal things, don't you? Things like gold pins and money clips, knives inlaid with mother of pearl...and gold bracelets with musical notes dangling from them. Maybe you like to hold on to them so you can use them against people in the future. What is it you had against Barry? Or should I ask, what is it he had on you? They found Alfie's pen on him around the time you were taking your final exams in school. Did it have something to do with that? Did he catch you cheating, Cal?"

Calvin's jaw went taut and his eyes narrowed with contempt. "I think both of you need to leave right now. Unless of course, I'm under arrest?"

"We know you weren't acting alone Mr. Clemont," Detective Prescott pressed. "In fact, you may be guilty of nothing more than aiding and abetting, something I'm sure the prosecutor will be willing to take into account if you served as a witness against the person who really killed Mary that night."

Penelope noted he was remaining silent on the subject of David Cranberry, for which she still couldn't think of a motive. Maybe it had to do with why Mary had been killed. If they could get him to confess with whom he had been working, that might answer everything.

As it was, they had him tangled up by a simple lighter. Penelope had been bluffing when she claimed that Andrew had last seen it the night of the storm. He had suggested Mary might have stolen some things before she left— perhaps including his gold lighter—which could only have happened that night.

"I'm not saying another word," Calvin said. "And if this is all you have, you have nothing—no motive, not even means or opportunity, not really. Maybe I found the lighter on the ground somewhere? As for conspiring with Ruth or anyone else in her family, you have even less evidence."

"Very well, Mr. Clemont." Detective Prescott walked back toward the door. Penelope watched him, feeling incredulous. Still, she couldn't very well stay if he was leaving. She had no authority to be there, and Calvin had officially kicked them out.

Once in the hallway, Calvin was quick to shut the door

behind them. Penelope followed Richard down to the first floor.

"Isn't there anything that we can do? After all, I called his bluff about the lighter."

Richard gave her an admiring smile. "That you did, and it was fairly ingenious of you."

Despite her frustration, Penelope felt a reluctant smile come to her face. "I took a stab and it happened to hit the right spot. Too bad it didn't result in the kill." She blinked in surprise and gave him a sheepish smile. "So to speak."

"Still, we can use it. If we can just figure out which of the Whitley family let him into the house that night, we can find out with whom he was conspiring, maybe even use them against each other to get an actual confession."

"Which of them do you think it could be?"

He sighed. "I honestly have no idea. Ruth would have been the obvious choice. But getting one man to do the killing and another to move the body? That makes no sense. Why not get one to do both at the same time?"

"What about the least obvious choices?" Pen offered. "Either William or Tallulah. William is hardly likely to conspire with one of Ruth's *gentleman friends*. The same is true of Tallulah. I have a feeling she's been kept on a short leash. When would she have an opportunity to conspire with Calvin? Also, there's something rather unseemly about being involved with one of your sister's paramours," she said wrinkling her nose.

"That just brings us back to Andrew. Sometimes the most likely suspect is the suspect."

"We might as well talk to William and Tallulah first since they are so close, just across the park."

"A good idea, it might save us the trouble if we're lucky."

They walked through the park to the Whitley home and were met with a bit of commotion already at their front door. William was standing in the doorway with his arms crossed as a covered form on a stretcher was being carried out by two men. He saw Penelope and Richard and glared at them.

"It seems *pater familias* has finally passed," Pen said under her breath.

William stormed down the steps to meet them, looking perfectly irate. "I hope you're happy, detective, Miss Banks. You finally managed to achieve it, *killing* my father. Whatever questions you have for me or the rest of my family, wherever they might be, will have to wait until *after* the funeral. Otherwise, I'm going to lodge a formal complaint."

He stormed back into the house and shut the door.

"And so it would seem the case has come to a stall."

"Not quite," said Penelope looking further down the sidewalk. Ducky and Mona were standing just outside their front door staring at the activity taking place on their street. "I think we can find one or two people to question in the meantime."

CHAPTER THIRTY

THE LOOKS OF APPREHENSION ON THE FACES OF DUCKY and Mona deepened as Penelope and Richard approached the Bishop home.

"I missed you last night at the party," Penelope remarked.

"Yes, well, I thought it prudent that I start limiting my....more frivolous activities. After all, I only just returned to New York. I'm going to be a married man, it's time I gave up all those shenanigans and settled down like a proper husband."

Pen recalled what Walter had said about Ducky's parents cutting him off. She couldn't blame him for trying to get back into their good graces by avoiding a late-night party among the bohemian artist set. The reality of being broke had obviously hit Ducky hard.

"Yes, well that was probably for the best, after all, there was another murder. And coincidentally enough, at least two members of the Whitley family were there."

"Surely you don't *still* suspect any of them of murder, do you? Really Pen, at this point it's becoming harassment.

I've known them all my life and they could hardly do something as undignified as commit murder."

"I've found that anyone is capable of it. It's too bad you weren't there to once again dissuade me from the idea of murder as you have been doing this entire week. This time there was not only a body but also a murder weapon, so there's no denying it."

"Just stop this, Penelope. Today of all days you want to bring up murder again. Mr. Whitley's body has only just been taken away."

"Well, he'll be the third body this week, won't he?"

"Oh, do stop!" Mona protested her hand coming up to pinch her forehead. "You know how upsetting I find all this talk of death."

"See, you've gone and upset Mona. If the Whitleys did have it in mind to file a complaint against you, I'm afraid I'd have no choice but to serve as a witness. I'm sorry Penelope, I've always thought you were a fun gal, but perhaps it's time you grow up and settle down as well."

Penelope studied him. She might have believed this change in him if she hadn't seen him be perfectly delinquent the night of the storm. Today, he might as well have been William Whitley himself.

"*Zounds*, he's paying you, isn't he?"

The instant look of panic on Ducky's face told her she was right. "That's why you've been acting so reluctant." She glared at Ducky's fiancée. "And why Mona told Walter to keep quiet about what he saw. It's William, isn't it? It has to be. He's been controlling this whole thing from the beginning."

"We have no idea what you're talking about," Mona insisted, glaring at Penelope.

"Need I remind you about laws regarding obstructing

justice," Detective Prescott said next to her. "If you have information regarding either murder you are obligated to inform the police."

"We don't know anything about a murder," Ducky protested.

"I can very easily get a warrant for your financial accounts. There is no privilege when it comes to banking information. It wouldn't be too hard to lay a charge of conspiracy on you."

Mona looked on the verge of tears and Ducky looked aghast.

"Alright, alright. Mind you, we didn't do anything illegal. William *never* confessed to murder, in fact, he insisted he had nothing to do with anything of the sort."

"I'm sure he did," Penelope said in a sardonic voice.

"He's only trying to protect his family, Pen, as he should," Ducky said placing an arm around his future wife. "You don't understand the pressure he's been under, having to take over when Mr. Whitley became ill. He's been shut out of most of his father's business because the man refuses to give up control even from his sick bed. All the while, William has to serve as the stand-in father to siblings who refuse to grow up. Ruth, has no boundaries whatsoever, gallivanting around with any young man in Washington Square who catches her eye. Andrew is still feckless as ever with his silly dreams of producing on Broadway. Tallulah is once again in love with the wrong man. William would much rather be starting his own family but he can't, can he? Now you want to dredge up this business about murder, sullying their good name!"

"None of what you said absolves him of murder. In fact, it only makes him more likely to—" Penelope paused. "Wait a second. *Tallulah?*"

"What about her?" Ducky asked impatiently.

"You said she's in love with someone—someone other than the piano player?"

"Apparently."

"Who is it?"

"I have no idea. William doesn't even know. But all the signs are apparently there. He's caught her leaving the home without telling anyone where she's going. There've also been secret phone calls, and so on."

"Zounds! How in the world did I miss it? Of course, the signs were there!"

Detective Prescott quirked one eyebrow up in curiosity.

"Thank you, Ducky, you've been more than helpful," Penelope said with a satisfied smile. Ducky didn't look at all happy about that.

Penelope took Richard's arm and led him further down the block so she could speak with him away from prying ears.

"I know that look. What is it?"

"Tallulah was the one working with Calvin."

"How do you figure?"

"Certain things that on their own either didn't mean much or I misread. That day when she was staring out at the park. I thought she was looking wistfully at the children, thinking about the ones she wouldn't have with her piano player. But who else was in the park that day?"

"The law students."

"Specifically Calvin. It was him she was staring at. Then, later on when we caught up to her, the look on her face when she talked about Ruth's indiscretions with the law students? I thought she was just being priggish at how loose her sister's morals were. In retrospect that was a look of resentment, maybe even jealousy on her face."

Richard gave a conceding nod.

"It all makes sense now. It didn't take too much prodding for her to reveal everything about what she overheard between William and Mary. I think she resents him, almost as much as she does her father. Ruth said he was practically a twin of their father. She was far too adamant that William hadn't killed Mary, all the while feeding us incriminating information about him that she knew we would follow up on. She may have even purposely left the body in such an open location in the hopes that Mary *would* be discovered. Having heard William's conversation, she knew the woman wasn't really her cousin, so she had nothing to fear regarding the will. She hadn't counted on Ruth coming along to move the body afterwards."

"It makes sense, but this is all just supposition. I can't very well get any kind of warrant based on a stare or look of resentment, even a hearsay conversation."

"The bracelet. Do you remember her answer when we asked if Mary was still wearing the bracelet when she left?"

"Yes...she said she hadn't been wearing it. That William probably took it back."

"So how did it get into Thomas's apartment? Tallulah must have invited Mary back in after William kicked her out. She murdered her, then made a frantic call to Calvin to come help her with the body. That's when he stole Andrew's lighter. Then, he or both of them moved the body to the fountain, where he also took Mary's bracelet. He was probably the one who Walter saw running south into the trees. Either the lightning or Ducky's idiotic proclamation must have spooked him. They had probably been counting on the darkness of the broken lamp to mask them as they placed the body. Maybe Cal had the idea of framing Thomas with the bracelet when he took it, knowing that

Ruth was with him after she left his apartment. Maybe that idea came later...like when he trapped us on the roof."

"We just need to confirm with William Whitley that she did indeed have the bracelet on when she left. At this point, I'm sure a complaint will land in my file, but I don't care. Let's go. "

Two of them marched back to the Whitley home and knocked on the door. When the maid answered, Richard insisted that she call William to the door and he wouldn't take no for an answer. The oldest Whitley sibling was understandably even more irate when he finally made an appearance in the doorway.

"At this point, detective I've had about enough of—"

"We just have one question for you and then we'll leave you alone," Penelope interrupted. "It's a simple yes or no answer, one that could put an end to this and take the blame away from you."

"What is it?" He asked begrudgingly, no doubt thrilled at the prospect of putting an end to this.

"Let's step outside. I don't want to bother the rest of your family with this," Detective Prescott suggested.

Though he still looked disgruntled, he followed them a few feet away from the home. "Well, get on with it."

Penelope turned to Detective Prescott to ask the question, *officially*.

"When you turned Mary Tate out of your house, was she still wearing the bracelet you had given her, the gold one with a music note?"

"Well, it certainly wasn't worth the trouble of taking back at that point. Yes, she still had it on. Is that it, the *one* question you wanted to ask?"

"It is, thank you."

William gave them a quizzical look, then shook his head with impatience and stormed back to his home.

"Well, there you have it, detective. Tallulah lied."

"It seems a third Whitley is going to be a guest of the New York Police Department."

"And William Whitley may very well join his father, toes up, once he learns as much."

They both turned to stare at the Whitley residence.

"Should we wait until after the funeral?" Penelope asked.

"Something tells me there isn't much love lost between the Whitley children and their father. I think we should do Tallulah the favor of not having to attend his funeral and question her right now."

"I agree," said Penelope.

They both approached the Whitley house once again.

CHAPTER THIRTY-ONE

It took another round of demanding and insisting to get past the maid and then William Whitley. However, eventually, a surprisingly calm and willing Tallulah appeared in the doorway to greet them, despite the objections of her brother.

"How can I help you, detective, Miss Banks?"

"Miss Whitley, we just have a few questions for you," Detective Prescott said.

Tallulah studied them both for a moment. Now, Penelope could see it, the cunning behind those serene blue eyes that seemed so innocent, even filled with trepidation before now. It was a shame, Tallulah would have made an excellent poker player.

"Of course detective, anything you need."

"Tallulah!" William protested. "I insist you go back inside this instant!"

She ignored him, a brief look of smug satisfaction whispering across her face as she ignored his demand and followed Penelope and Detective Prescott out.

It wasn't lost on either Penelope or Richard.

They led her across the street to Washington Square Park where they found a bench to sit on in private. Tallulah sat in between Richard and Penelope with a polite smile now plastered on her face.

There was no point in being coy about things at that point, so Penelope decided to be perfectly frank. "How long have you and Calvin been seeing one another"

Tallulah's smile grew slightly, which meant she had been expecting that question. "I have no idea what you mean, Miss Banks."

"He's already told us most of it," Penelope lied.

Tallulah's mouth pursed with sly amusement. "I seriously doubt that. *If* indeed there was anything *to* tell."

Penelope realized that Ruth was an amateur compared to her older sister when it came to having men wrapped around her finger. Tallulah seemed far too sure of herself. Maybe she had learned her lesson after falling so hard for the piano player who had jilted her.

"We do have evidence, Andrew's gold lighter, the one he lost the night of the storm. I saw Cal with it the next morning. There's only one way he could have gotten it—if he was inside your home, which meant someone had to let him in."

It was the ever so subtle twitch in her eye when Penelope mentioned the lighter that gave it away. It was smoothly replaced by the cool look she gave Penelope.

"Calvin is one of Ruth's little friends, isn't he? She must have been the one to let him in. After all, she would have a key."

"Why did you tell us that Mary wasn't wearing the bracelet that night when she left?" Detective Prescott said, joining in. "We have confirmation that she *was* actually wearing it at that point."

"I must have been mistaken. I've been so preoccupied with my poor, ill father, I'm sure I can't remember what I had for breakfast." A look of wretched sorrow came to her face, as though teasing them with the very defense she planned on making should they arrest her. She was a maestra at work. Penelope almost admired it. Almost.

"Did you know Ruth and Thomas were on the roof of his apartment building that night? Looking out at the park. They've confessed to moving the body after seeing *you* place her there. You've been caught, Tallulah. We don't need a confession."

Tallulah laughed. "Now, I know you're lying."

"Oh?" Penelope said arching an eyebrow. "So it was all Calvin's doing, then? Because according to *him* you were right there with him after *you* stabbed her. We're talking to you now simply as a courtesy, a chance to tell your side of the story."

"He never said such a thing." Tallulah didn't look *quite* so sure of herself now.

Penelope laughed softly, now knowing exactly how to twist the screw. "Surely, you should know better than to trust men by now, especially when they have enough *motivation* to protect their own interests above yours. Just like with Reggie the piano player, who felt money was more important than marrying you."

"That won't work," Tallulah said, though Penelope noted the way her hands fisted her skirts.

"Do you really trust that Calvin would risk going to prison just to save your skin? How long do you think he'll hold up before he breaks and places all the blame on you. After all, you're the only one with a motive."

"This isn't working," Tallulah gritted out, staring ahead with eyes like granite.

"He doesn't strike me as being *that* much in love with you, not when he's been playing around with Ruth this whole time—that very night, in fact. What were they up to in his apartment before you called? Your own sister, Tallulah. I'll bet they had a good laugh over it. Him playing the tomcat while you remained the perfect little spinster, catering to the father who once ruined your life. And now a brother who was doing the same. Was he the one who forced you to care for your father? A job his wife could have easily done. And now the future handsome, wealthy attorney you were pinning your hopes on couldn't even keep his hands off your sister."

"Stop it!" Tallulah said, seething as she began to unravel.

"We know he was in the house that night, and that it was you who let him in." Detective Prescott said. "We just need to know who did the actual killing."

"He did it, Calvin was the one who killed her," Tallulah spat out with a sneer.

Penelope quickly met Richard's eyes and saw the satisfaction in them. They had her. She turned her attention back to Tallulah who was still talking.

"I was worried about what I'd heard Mary threaten William with. I feared she might somehow get in touch with father and then all the money would be lost. I was only looking out for my siblings." Tallulah had reverted back to the timid, innocent woman Pen had first seen. She knew it was just an act, but she certainly wasn't going to keep Tallulah from talking. "I just wanted to talk to her, maybe persuade her somehow. I knew Calvin could help with that, he was going to be an attorney, after all. Then he pulled out the knife, the one he stole from his friend, George. He liked to brag about that, how his friends had no idea he'd been the one to take all their things, how he'd set up his other friend, Barry after he'd caught him cheating on an exam."

Penelope blinked in surprise. That placed the murder weapon used to kill David Cranberry in Calvin's hands. Tallulah was certainly going scorched earth.

"I didn't realize until too late that he had stabbed her. He was the one to suggest moving her to the fountain and did that part himself." Suddenly tears came to her eyes and her hand came up, pressing into her chest. "I was too scared to say anything, scared of what he might do to me if I told. He told me if I ever said a word, he would kill me too. That's why I lied about the bracelet, I knew he had taken it."

Tallulah seemed to have an answer for every potential accusation. And all of them pointed directly at Calvin. Penelope wasn't buying it.

"Did he tell you why he killed David Cranberry?"

Tallulah shook her head and shrugged. "No."

Penelope tilted her head to consider her. "You don't seem surprised that he's dead. Did you hear about his murder from someone already? How do you even know the name?"

Tallulah blinked, the tears stopping as she considered her response. "What do you mean?"

"I mean there's no way you could have heard about his murder. Andrew and Ruth are both in jail. If I had just found out the man I was involved with had killed a second person, my first reaction would be shock. Yours is a simple shrug of the shoulders. Did Cal call you and tell you about it?"

Tallulah stared at her, a pitiful look coming to her face once again. "Yes, he did. He called to boast about it, to try and use it as leverage to further silence me."

"So he called you this morning? Or was it late last

night?" Penelope made a point of looking around Tallulah to give Richard a questioning look. "I'm sure the phone company keeps records of every connected call that's made, correct? You could get a warrant to see those records, no?"

Pen had no idea if this was true, but Richard blessedly played along."Correct. In fact, we could get a record for any calls made the night of the murder as well, now that we know which numbers to ask for. They can also tell us who was calling whom."

Suddenly the tears were fully gone and Tallulah completely dropped any pretense. The way she transitioned into a cunning vixen took even Penelope by surprise.

"There's no way either of you would be able to pin *David's* murder on me. I was at home that night, *all* night. If Calvin got it into his head that David Cranberry needed to be killed, that has nothing to do with me," she said with a smug smile.

"Except for motive, of which he has none. Except, of course, his connection to you. Like Mary, David knew the truth about the Whitley children and your devious methods of getting more than your share of the inheritance. He needed to be silenced too, didn't he?"

Tallulah cut her eyes to Penelope. "*Or*...maybe Calvin was simply a jealous lover. Maybe he saw David at my house that morning with the bouquet of flowers, and he assumed they were meant for me. How was Calvin to know that silly man was there to see some woman he'd met on a train?"

"And I'm sure you did nothing to relieve him of those fears did you?"

Tallulah's only response was a self-satisfied smirk. She just couldn't help herself.

"You really are devious," Pen said in awe.

"You're also guilty of at best, aiding and abetting, at worst conspiring to commit murder," Detective Prescott said.

Tallulah's face went blank. The only signs that she was worried or angry were her lips tightening in anger. Still, there was a certain look of defiant satisfaction on her face.

"I wouldn't look so smug if I were you, Tallulah. If Calvin is weak enough to do your bidding, he'll be weak enough to cave. He isn't the kind of man cut out for prison time, and he knows it. He'll do everything he can to save his neck, even if it means betraying you."

Something flickered in Tallulah's gaze, telling Pen she was coming to the same conclusion. Either way, they finally knew who killed David Cranberry, and at least conspired to kill Mary Tate.

"Miss Whitley, will you please stand," Detective Prescott said as he rose from the bench. "I'm placing you under arrest for your connection to the murder of Mary Tate."

Penelope rose as well and looked past Detective Prescott as he led Tallulah away. Her eyes landed on The Row, with its stately and dignified facade. It was a firm reminder that facades were just that, facades. They could hide a number of devious schemes and murderous intent.

Of course, Washington Square Park was no different. Penelope turned her attention first to the iconic arch and then to the fountain. The usual characters were up to their usual cheerful summer routines—running around, making art, playing music, having conversations, engaged in debates —all blissfully ignorant of the dark past of the park they were in, the remnants of which lay right beneath their feet.

Perhaps facades were a good thing. Let the dead rest in peace; let the living go on living.

CHAPTER THIRTY-TWO

Several days later, Penelope was in her office. That morning she was engaged in putting out a small fire over the telephone as Jane pretended not to overhear.

"Well, we can't very well keep Emma from quitting, Cousin Cordelia."

"I don't see why not! Whatever happened to loyalty among servants? She comes into a tidy sum of money from some aunt she barely knew and suddenly being a maid is too good for her?"

"You should be happy for her. She's allowed to live her life the way she pleases. Now she has the money to do it."

"Bah! Cuba, she said. Can you believe that? Flitting away her days with rum drinks on hot beaches. I can't think of anything more miserable."

"I can think of at least a few more miserable things."

"You aren't being helpful, Penelope. Oh, whatever am I to do? Everyone is abandoning me. You with your *job*, and now this. Where is my medicine when I need it?"

"I haven't abandoned you. In fact, I'll pick up some of

your, *ahem*, medicine before coming home tonight. I may even share some with you. How does that sound?"

Penelope saw Jane stifle a smile, knowing exactly what that "medicine" was. Pen shot her a conspiratorial wink.

"Bless you, Penelope. You're the only one who cares about me at all."

"I'm sure that's not true. Chives and Arabella haven't abandoned you and they surely care about you."

"Oh, I suppose you're right."

The sound of the door opening to the front office carried through. Jane quickly rose from her desk to go greet whoever had just entered.

"Cousin, I have to go now. It seems I have a client."

"Yes, yes, you and your *career*. In my day, women didn't do such things. Modern times, Penelope, they'll be the death of me soon enough."

"Well, not too soon I hope."

She smiled as she hung up. It brightened when she saw who had just entered the office.

"Susan!" Pen said, gesturing to the chair across from her. "What brings you here?"

"I hope I didn't interrupt anything. I heard you on the phone."

"Oh, that was nothing. It seems I've lost yet another maid, which is nothing new for me. But enough about me, how are you? I know how trying this must have all been for you. Is there something I can do for you?"

"I must confess, it was mostly curiosity that brought me by. I was quite intrigued when I discovered you had your own private investigator business. I just had to come and see it for myself. It really is quite something." She took a moment to look around with admiration at the modern art deco office, then brought her attention back to Penelope.

"As for me, I'm perfectly fine. It's mostly my cousins I'm concerned for."

"How considerate of you," Pen said diplomatically. She wasn't so sure she would have been quite so generous in her thoughts about any scheming cousins.

With Walter's confirmation that there had in fact been a body, an official case was opened. According to Detective Prescott, it had taken less than an hour for Calvin to reveal that Tallulah had been the one to do the stabbing with a letter opener, at least when it came to Mary Tate. As Penelope had surmised, she *had* wanted to frame her older brother for the crime and had sought out the help of the man she'd been secretly having a relationship with for months. He had claimed he'd maintained a casual relationship with Ruth so as not to raise any suspicion.

Pen believed that about as much as she suspected Ruth and Tallulah did.

Tallulah had thus felt no qualms about confessing that she had put the idea in Calvin's head that David Cranberry was a contender for her affections. No doubt she considered him a loose end that needed snipping. Calvin had used George's knife in order to frame him. In fact, that seemed to be his modus operandi when it came to stealing things. Alfie had mentioned that he was competitive, which was quite the understatement.

Ruth and Thomas had pleaded guilty to a lesser sentence rather than go to trial. They confessed that they had eventually moved the body to the Hudson River, so as to never be found. Calvin and Tallulah were taking their chances with trials.

At least the two former law students wouldn't have to worry about taking the bar exam. Ever.

As for the two sisters, who knew?

Mary Tate's only living relative was an uncle who hadn't seen her since she was a child. He had mostly expressed his relief that he wouldn't be obligated to pay for any burial expenses, which Penelope thought rather unseemly. As such, Jane and she had held a short vigil near the river in her honor, feeling that someone should at least acknowledge her passing in a respectful manner.

"Yes, I suppose this has all ended on a much more tragic note than I expected when I first arrived in New York. I feel just terrible about what happened to poor Mary, I'll be sure to pray for her. Still, I want to focus on something positive coming out of all of this. I've finally met my cousins, which is nice. I plan on visiting more often, despite everything. Hopefully, that will make up for their disappointment."

"Disappointment?"

"Yes, well..." Susan paused before continuing. "It would seem my uncle didn't have quite as much to leave as they might have hoped for."

"Oh?" Pen repeated, now much more curious. She could see Jane perking up with interest as well.

"It seems his business wasn't as...robust, as he might have led William to believe. Perhaps that's why he insisted on maintaining control even while sick. I suspect it was his pride at work. Everything has been paid for via loans and debt. When all is said and done there may only be about a thousand dollars left."

"You don't say!" Pen exclaimed. She saw Jane's eyes go wide with similar shock.

"Even Mr. Willis said he had been working pro bono because he didn't believe in abandoning a client, and most of the work had already been done. Fortunately, the lease on the home is paid through the end of the year, so Andrew, William, and Caroline will have a place to live as they get their affairs in order. I'll of course come back to visit, just to see how they are getting on; especially Tallulah and Ruth, who I think may need it most. Family is family after all. I don't want any more division among us, even when it comes to something like murder."

Pen thought about Cousin Cordelia, who, as needy and fretful as she was, had also been there for her once upon a time when she was most in need, and had certainly never used Pen in the way the Whitleys had. Perhaps she'd get an extra large bottle of "medicine" for them to share tonight.

This also made Pen think of her own somewhat estranged father. Over the past year—ironically because of Pen's profession, of which he most certainly did *not* approve —their relationship was slowly beginning to thaw.

"Despite the unfortunate circumstances, I'm glad to have met you, Susan," Pen said truthfully.

"I'm glad to have met you too, Penelope. I hope you'll allow me to write to you in the future? I'd be curious to hear about the cases you are working on. I suspect they might make for interesting stories for me to write, maybe even into a book one day."

"Of course," Pen said, "I'd love that."

They heard the door to the front office open. Before Jane could make it out to greet their new visitor, he walked in of his own accord.

"Oh, I'm sorry, I didn't realize you had a client," he said, removing his hat.

"Alfie!" Pen greeted. "Don't worry. In fact, this is rather fortuitous. This is Susan Bennett, the woman at the middle of all the hullabaloo that's happened over the last week. Susan, this is Alfred, who inadvertently helped me solve the case."

His brow shot up in surprise. "Oh, well that is fascinating. Pleased to meet you, Miss Bennett."

"You as well," she said before rising. "I should leave you to it."

Susan made her goodbyes to everyone and left.

"I didn't mean to interrupt," Alfred said apologetically. "I just wanted to congratulate you. It's always a fine thing when justice is served. Even Barry has gotten his. NYU has reinstated him and allowed him to retake his final exams to graduate, just in time to take the bar."

"Wonderful, though I'm sure this business with your other friends was no doubt upsetting."

"Actually, learning the worst about people, even those I was close to, prepares me for my future career. No one is without fault, and everyone deserves a good defense."

"I suppose I can't argue with that."

Pen sensed there was something more he wanted, the way he fiddled with his hat. He finally spun around to face Jane.

"I'm glad to see you looking well today."

"Why, thank you," Jane said, giving him a bewildered, but pleased smile.

It was obvious that Jane had no idea who he was, which Pen found decidedly amusing. It was also obvious that Alfred had come mostly to see Jane again, which Pen found even more amusing. He hadn't seemed all that impressed with the drunken mess he had carried out of the Golden Swan.

"Do we know each other Mr...?"

"Paisley. Alfred Paisley."

"My, what a lovely last name—oh!" Jane suddenly gasped, her hand coming to her mouth in horror. Her cheeks turned into perfect tomatoes when she suddenly recognized him. "Oh...oh, my!"

"Don't be upset, Miss—Jane." Alfie pushed his glasses up his nose. "You look quite nice today. Lovely even."

Jane's hand slowly lowered. "I must apologize for that night, Mr. Paisley. I wasn't myself at all. In fact, I'm never like that."

"My fault entirely," Pen sang out. "I should have remembered her low tolerance for alcohol."

"Something for which you have nothing to apologize," he assured her.

"Thank you," Jane said, her cheeks now pink for altogether different reasons.

They stood there, staring at each other to the point that Penelope wondered if they had completely forgotten she was in the room.

Not that she minded, of course.

She had a good feeling about these two.

Almost as much as Pen herself had about Richard Prescott. With whom she finally had a proper date for dinner.

EPILOGUE

"Delmonico's?" Pen said, looking across the table at Richard. "I certainly didn't expect you to go this far when it came to our first dinner."

He grinned back at her. "Well, I had to follow up a pretty spectacular kiss, and a pretty spectacular dessert with an equally spectacular dinner."

Pen laughed. "They were pretty spectacular, I have to say."

"Of course, the company is what makes it so."

'Yes," she said, feeling suddenly self-conscious. She idly pushed an imaginary hair back behind her ear.

Richard laughed softly. "At least now I know what tell to look for if I'm ever dumb enough to challenge you to a game of poker."

"What?"

"That move of yours. I can always tell when I make you nervous or self-conscious."

Penelope laughed. "Well, I suppose that makes us even. I can easily tell when you're particularly exasperated with me. You take your hat off and run your hand through your hair."

"It's a wonder I have any hair left."

"Oh stop," she said with a laugh. "Tell me right now that you don't secretly enjoy it when you find out I'm involved in a case with you and I'll get up and walk out right now."

"Being that we've already ordered and I'll have to pay for the meals, either way, I suppose I shouldn't have you running off too soon."

"It would take quite a bit to make me run off, detective," she said.

"Good," he replied, studying her. "I like having you near me."

"Don't speak too soon, you've only just peeled the first layer from me. Wait a while."

"That sounds ominous."

"You should know by now not to be surprised when you find yourself surprised by me."

"True," he said, arching an eyebrow. "So tell me, what should I be surprised by next?"

She laughed. "That would ruin the surprise."

He grinned. "Not even a hint?"

"Well, my birthday is coming up. I'll be turning twenty-five."

"Yes, I know."

"And I plan on throwing a party."

"Mmm-hmm."

"At Agnes's mansion in Long Island."

"Yes," he said, becoming suddenly wary.

"And I really should do her memory justice."

"I see." His brow creased with concern. By now, he was quite familiar with Agnes Sterling's infamous parties.

"Didn't the clause in her will dictate that you share a lease on the mansion with the other named parties?"

"Nothing I have planned violates that. It did state we were allowed guests, and there was no stipulation as to how many. I have access to the home for another six months and it deserves a party that is worthy of her memory. Besides, they're hardly in a position to protest, are they?"

A begrudging smile came to his face and he conceded that with a nod. "How much should I be worried about this party?"

Penelope couldn't help the devilish grin that came to her face. "Have you read this new book that was just published by F. Scott Fitzgerald called *The Great Gatsby*?"

CONTINUE ON FOR YOUR FREE BOOK!

AUTHOR'S NOTE

This book was sparked by a walking tour of New York I decided to take one day on a lark. (shout out to the Gangsters and Ghosts Tour of New York).

The infamous 1917 break-in of the Washington Square Arch is apparently one of New York's best kept, yet well-known secrets. From my research, it happened almost word for word as Benny described in this book, including the fact that the door was unlocked! (Note: this is obviously no longer the case.)

As for the rest of Washington Square Park's macabre history, it is also indeed true. From a potter's field to the hanging grounds of the post-Revolutionary War, it does have its dark past, and yes, supposedly many a bone was unearthed during the construction of the fountain and the various pathways. The rumor is, they have not all been removed....

By far the most fascinating bit of research I happened upon was learning about the Black and Tan saloons of the city. Washington Square has always served as what one might call the Great Divide between various classes in New York. In the mid-17th century freed slaves were allowed to farm south of that area, mostly to serve as a buffer between the potentially dangerous indigenous tribes and the rest of the city. The area southeast of the park remained mostly populated by African-Americans well into the early 20th century, earning it the moniker Little Africa.

Being that de facto segregation was always one-sided, the bars and saloons that did business in the area were open to all, and in fact, became infamous establishments for inter-racial socializing and colorful, open-minded discourse. It was the famous muckraking journalist, Jacob Riis who coined the term "Black and Tan" in his famous book *How the Other Half Lives* (1890), causing a stir as intended.

The Golden Swan, one of the most famous Black and Tan saloons (where the original 1917 Arch trespassers spent many an evening) was a real establishment run by the former boxer Thomas Wallace. I took a few liberties in my descriptions, being that there isn't much information I could find about what happened to the establishment post-Prohibition. Currently, there is a small garden on that corner of 6th and 4th with a Golden Swan Garden placard marking its location.

I do try to keep specific businesses or addresses out of my books unless they are iconic or famous (e.g. Delmonico's & The Golden Swan). The Row along Washington Square Park North is an actual row of Georgian-era homes that were built in 1833. Until New York University began recently buying most of them, they were owned by Sailor's Snug Harbor and leased to residents, never sold.

As a final note, (and in the interest of transparency and honesty) the "desperately seeking Susan" bit was a blatant rip from the movie of the same name. Who doesn't love a good Madonna reference?

Until the next book, thanks for reading!

CONTINUE ON FOR YOUR FREE BOOK!

GET YOUR FREE BOOK!

Mischief at The Peacock Club

**A bold theft at the infamous Peacock Club.
Can Penelope solve it to save her own neck?**

1924 New York

Penelope "Pen" Banks has spent the past two years making
ends meet by playing cards. It's another Saturday night at
The Peacock Club, one of her favorite haunts, and she has

her sites set on a big fish, who just happens to be the special guest of the infamous Jack Sweeney.

After inducing Rupert Cartland, into a game of cards, Pen thinks it just might be her lucky night. Unfortunately, before the night ends, Rupert has been robbed—his diamond cuff links, ruby pinky ring, gold watch, and wallet...all gone!

With The Peacock Club's reputation on the line, Mr. Sweeney, aided by the heavy hand of his chief underling Tommy Callahan, is holding everyone captive until the culprit is found.

For the promise of a nice payoff, not to mention escaping the club in one piece, Penelope Banks is willing to put her unique mind to work to find out just who stole the goods.

This is a prequel novella to the *Penelope Banks Murder Mysteries* series, taking place at The Peacock Club before Penelope Banks became a private investigator.

Access your book at the link below:
https://dl.bookfunnel.com/4sv9fir4h3

ALSO BY COLETTE CLARK

PENELOPE BANKS MURDER MYSTERIES

A Murder in Long Island

The Missing White Lady

Pearls, Poison & Park Avenue

Murder in the Gardens

A Murder in Washington Square

The Great Gaston Murder

A Murder After Death

ABOUT THE AUTHOR

Colette Clark lives in New York and has always enjoyed learning more about the history of her amazing city. She decided to combine that curiosity and love of learning with her addiction to reading and watching mysteries. Her first series, **Penelope Banks Murder Mysteries** is the result of those passions. When she's not writing she can be found doing Sudoku puzzles, drawing, eating tacos, visiting museums dedicated to unusual/weird/wacky things, and, of course, reading mysteries by other great authors.

Join my Newsletter to receive news about New Releases and Sales!
http://eepurl.com/hTR4RH

Printed in Great Britain
by Amazon